In Case We're Separated

In Case We're Separated

CONNECTED STORIES

Alice Mattison

wm

WILLIAM MORROW

An Imprint of HarperCollins*Publishers*

Some of these stories appeared in the following journals and anthologies:

"In Case We're Separated," *Ploughshares, Best American Short Stories*
"I Am Not Your Mother," *Ploughshares, The Pushcart Prize*
"In the Dark, Who Pats the Air," *Shenandoah*
"Brooklyn Sestina," *Michigan Quarterly Review*
"Election Day," *Michigan Quarterly Review*
"The Bad Jew," *Glimmer Train*
"Future House," *Glimmer Train*
"Pastries at the Bus Stop," *Ms. Magazine*
"The Odds It Would Be You," *The Threepenny Review*

HarperCollins books may be purchased for educational, business, or sales promotional use. For information please write: Special Markets Department, HarperCollins Publishers, 10 East 53rd Street, New York, NY 10022.

FIRST EDITION

Designed by Stephanie Huntwork

Printed on acid-free paper

Library of Congress Cataloging-in-Publication Data

Mattison, Alice.
    In case we're separated : connected stories / Alice Mattison.—1st ed.
        p.   cm.
    ISBN-13: 978-0-06-621377-4
    ISBN-10: 0-06-621377-0
    1. Domestic fiction, American.   2. Mothers and daughters—Fiction.
3. Grandmothers—Fiction.   I. Title.

PS3563.A8598I5   2005
813'.54—dc22

                                                        2005043422

05   06   07   08   09   WBC/QW   10   9   8   7   6   5   4   3   2   1

In memory of my mother, Rose Eisenberg

CONTENTS

CONTENTS

In Case We're Separated

In Case We're Separated

You're a beautiful woman, sweetheart," Edwin Friend began. His girlfriend, Bobbie Kaplowitz, paid attention: Edwin rarely spoke up and complimented her. He tipped his chair against her sink and glanced behind him, but the drain board wasn't piled so high that the back of his head would start an avalanche today. He took a decisive drink from his glass of water and continued, "But in that particular dress you look fat."

It was a bright Saturday morning in October 1954. Edwin often visited Bobbie on Saturday mornings, and she had dressed up a little, anticipating. Now she didn't bother to speak. She reached behind to unfasten the hook and eye at the back of her neck, worked the zipper down without help, stepped out of the dress, and in her underwear took the sharp scissors. She cut a big piece of brown wrapping paper from a roll she kept next to the refrigerator, while Edwin said several times, "What are you doing?"

Bobbie folded the dress, which was chestnut brown with a rust-and-cream-colored arrowlike decoration that crossed her breasts and pointed fetchingly down. She set the folded dress in the middle of the paper, wrapped and taped it, and addressed the package to her slimmer sister in Pittsburgh. Then she went into the bedroom and changed into something seriously gorgeous.

"Come, Bradley," she called, though Edwin would have babysat, but Bradley came quickly. He was a thin six-year-old with dark curls and the habit of resting his hands on his hips, so from the front he looked slightly supervisory and from the back his pointed elbows stuck out like outlines of small wings. They left Edwin looking surprised. At the post office, a considerable walk away, the clerk said the package had to be tied with string, but lent Bobbie a big roll of twine and his scissors. Bobbie was wearing high-heeled shoes, and she braced herself on the counter with one gloved hand. She was short and the shoes made her wobble. She took the end of the twine in her mouth, grasped it between her teeth, and jerked her head back to pull it tight. It was brown twine, now reddened with her lipstick, and its taste was woody and dry. Fibers separating from the twine might travel across Bobbie's tongue and make her gag. For all she knew, her poor old teeth might loosen.

Much was brown: the twine, the paper around the package (even the dress inside if one could see it), and the wooden counter with its darkened brass decorations. The counter was old enough to have taken on the permanent sour coloring of wooden and metal objects in Brooklyn that had remained in one place—where any hand might close upon them—since the century turned. But Bobbie's lipstick, and the shoes she'd changed into, and her suit—which had a straight skirt with a kick pleat—were red. She wore a half-slip because she was a loose woman. Joke. Edwin's hands always went first to her bare, fleshy midriff. Then he seemed to enjoy urging the nylon petticoat down, sliding the rubber knobs up and out of the metal loops that attached her stockings to her girdle, even tugging the girdle off. She never let him take off her nylons because he wasn't careful.

Bobbie tied a firm knot. Then she changed her mind. She poked the roll of twine and the scissors toward the clerk with an apologetic wave, called to Bradley—who was hopping from one dark medallion on the tile floor to the next, flapping his arms—and went home. As Bobbie walked, one eye on Bradley, the package dangled from her finger on its string like a new purchase. At home she found Edwin taking apart her Sunbeam Mixmaster with her only tool, a rusty screwdriver.

"Didn't you say it wasn't working?" Edwin asked.

"There's nothing wrong with it. I didn't say anything."

Edwin was married. He had told Bobbie he was a bachelor who couldn't marry her because he lived with his mother, who was old, silly, and anti-Semitic. But his mother lived in her own apartment and was not silly or anti-Semitic as far as he knew. Edwin had a wife named Dorothy, a dental hygienist. She'd stopped working when their first child was born—they had two daughters—but sometimes she helped out her old boss. Now, fumbling to put Bobbie's mixer back together, Edwin began to wonder uneasily whether it wasn't Dorothy, dressing for work in her uniform, who happened to mention a broken mixer. He had never confused the two women before in the years he'd been Bobbie's boyfriend.

Edwin's monkey business had begun by mistake. He was a salesman for a baking supply company, and Bobbie was in charge of the payroll at a large commercial bakery. Though Edwin didn't wear a ring, he believed that everyone in the firms through which he passed assumed he was somebody's husband. However, a clerk in Bobbie's office had moved to Brooklyn from Minneapolis. When this young woman, who had distinctive habits, asked him straight out, Edwin misheard the question and said no. He had heard, "Mr. Friend, are you merry?"

Edwin was good-natured but not merry, and the question puzzled him until he found himself having lunch with Bobbie, to whom the young woman from Minneapolis had introduced him. He realized that he was on a date. Bobbie seemed eager and attractive, while Dorothy liked to make love about as often as she liked to order tickets and go to a Broadway show, or invite her whole family for dinner, and with about as much planning. Not knowing exactly what he had in mind, Edwin suggested that Bobbie meet him for a drink after work, nervous that she'd refuse anything less than dinner and a movie. But she agreed. Drinking a quick whiskey sour in a darkened lounge, she suggested that next time he come to her house. So his visits began: daytime conversations over a glass of water or a cup of coffee; suppers followed by bed. Bobbie was always interested. She only needed to make sure Bradley was sleeping.

Bobbie rarely spoke of her marriage. Her husband had been a tense, mumbly man, a printer. He'd remained aloof from her family. At first he said she was nothing like her crude relatives. "I felt refined, but I didn't like it," Bobbie told Edwin. Later her husband began to say she was *exactly* like her family, and at last he moved her and Bradley, an infant, into a dark two-room apartment where nothing worked and there was hardly ever any hot water. He said he slept at his shop, and at first he brought her money, but soon that stopped. "I didn't have enough hot water to bathe the baby," Bobbie said. "Let alone my whole self." Edwin imagined it: naked Bobbie clasping a thin baby and splashing warm water on herself from a chipped, shallow basin. She'd moved back with her mother and got a job. Eventually she could afford the apartment on Elton Street where Edwin now visited her. When Bradley was two she had taken him on the train to Reno, lived there for six weeks, and come home divorced, bringing her sisters silver pins and bracelets with Indian designs on them, arrows and stylized birds.

Bobbie's family wouldn't care much that Edwin wasn't Jewish, she assured him, and they'd understand that he couldn't be around often because of his mother. But they did want to know him. So Edwin had consented to an occasional Sunday lunch in Bobbie's kitchen with her mother or one of her sisters, eating whitefish and kippered salmon and bagels off a tablecloth printed with cherries, and watching the sun move across the table as the afternoon lengthened and he imagined Dorothy wondering. After the bagels they'd have coffee with marble cake from Bobbie's bakery. He'd tip his chair against the porcelain sink and consider how surprised his wife would be if she knew where he was, being polite to another woman's relatives. His own house was bigger and more up-to-date.

Dorothy would be even more surprised if she knew, right now, that Edwin was in that same kitchen, which was less sunny in the morning, fixing a mixer that wasn't broken. Edwin would have preferred to be a bigamist, not a deceiver. When he reassembled the mixer, it didn't work. He left the bowls and beaters and took the big contraption home in the trunk of his car. He'd work on it when Dorothy was out. She had promised Dr. Dressel, her old boss, a few hours in the coming week.

The day Edwin carried off the mixer, Bobbie's sister Sylvia and her kids, Joan and Richard, rang Bobbie's bell after lunch because they were all going to the Hayden Planetarium. Sylvia, a schoolteacher, had said, "Bradley's ready," as if she'd noticed blanks in his eyes where stars and planets belonged. Her own kids had often been to the planetarium. So the sisters walked to Fulton Street, urging along the children, who stamped on piles of brown sycamore leaves. Climbing the stairs to the elevated train, Bobbie was already tired. She'd have changed her shoes, but she liked the look of the red heels. They waited on the windy platform, Joan holding Bradley's hand tightly. She and Richard were tall, capable children who read signs out loud in firm voices: "No Spitting." "Meet Miss Subways." They had to change trains, and as the second one approached, Sylvia said, "Does Bradley know what to do in case we're separated?"

"Why should we get separated?" said Bobbie.

"It can always happen," Sylvia said as the doors opened. The children squeezed into one seat, and Sylvia leaned over them. She had short curly hair that was starting to go gray. "Remember," she said, "in case we get separated, if you're on the train, get off at the next stop and wait. And if you're on the platform, just wait where you are, and we'll come back for you. Okay?"

Joan and Richard were reaching across Bradley to slap each other's knees, but Bradley nodded seriously. Bobbie rarely offered directives like that, and he probably needed them, yet she felt irritated. At the planetarium, Bradley tried to read aloud words on the curved ceiling that was covered with stars. The theater darkened. While the stars revolved swiftly, a slightly spooky voice spoke of a time so far back that Bobbie felt disjoined from herself: she in her red suit would surely never happen. Anything at all might be true.

Then Bradley whispered something. "Do you have to go to the bathroom?" Bobbie asked. "I can't go in with you." If Edwin would marry her, he'd be there to take Bradley to the bathroom! The size of Bobbie's yearning, like the age of the stars, was suddenly clear. But Bradley shook his head. "No. No. I can't remember what I do if you get off the train without me."

"I wouldn't do that, honey," she said, but of course he continued to worry. She could feel his little worry machines whirring beside her.

"You scared him," she said to Sylvia as they shuffled toward the exit with the crowd, later. "About being lost on the subway."

"He needs to know," Sylvia said, and Bobbie wondered if Sylvia would be as bossy if she didn't have a husband, Louis—an accountant, a good man; although Sylvia said he was quick in bed.

They spent an hour in the natural history museum—where Joan held Bradley's hand, telling him what Bobbie hoped were nonfrightening facts—before taking the long subway ride home again. At the stop before theirs, Bradley suddenly stood and ran toward the closing doors, crying out. Richard tackled him, knocking him to the dirty floor, and Bobbie took him on her lap. Bradley had thought a departing back was hers. "Oh, sweetie," she said, brushing him off and kissing him. She carried him as far as the stairs.

"Well, I shouldn't have said anything," said Sylvia as they reached the sidewalk and turned toward home. The train's sound grew faint behind them.

Bobbie said nothing. If she agreed, Sylvia would change her mind and defend what she'd said after all. Bobbie glanced back at the three kids, who were counting something out loud in exultant voices—passing cars, maybe. "Seven! No, nine!"

"I have chopped meat," said Sylvia at last, when their silence had lasted for more than a block. "I'll make mashed potatoes. Lou will drive you, later, okay?"

"That would be nice," said Bobbie. They reached the corner of Sylvia's street and turned that way.

"Unless you have a date?" Sylvia added.

But it was cruel to make Bobbie say what was apparent. "No such luck."

"That guy has a problem," said Sylvia. "It's Saturday night!"

"Edwin says I look fat in that brown dress," Bobbie said. She never let herself think about Saturday nights. Edwin said his mother cooked corned beef and cabbage then, and minded if he went out. "Remember that dress? With the design down the front?"

"That gorgeous dress!" Sylvia said. "To tell the truth, you do look a little hefty in it, but who cares?"

In the dark, Bobbie cried. She hoped her sister would notice and maybe even put an arm around her, but that wasn't their way. Maybe Sylvia did notice. "I'll make a nice salad. You like salad, don't you?" she said soothingly.

Edwin's house was empty when he came home on Tuesday. Dorothy was working, and the girls were at a neighbor's. He spread newspaper on the dining-room table and fixed Dorothy's mixer, the one that had been broken in the first place. It was not badly broken. A wire was loose. Then it occurred to him that the mixers looked alike, with bulbous arms to hold the beaters, and curved white bases on which bowls rotated. He'd bought Dorothy's after seeing Bobbie's. Edwin set aside Dorothy's bowls and beaters. He carried Dorothy's fixed mixer out to his car, then returned and put Bobbie's broken one on the sheet of newspaper.

He jumped when he heard Dorothy and the girls arriving, but there was nothing to worry about. Dorothy asked, "Did you fix it?" and Edwin truthfully said, "Not yet." She stood behind him, watching as he took apart Bobbie's mixer. By this time it was hard to remember that the broken mixer was the one he had broken himself, not the one Dorothy had reported broken, and he listened attentively while she told him what she'd been about to mix when it didn't work. As he listened, his back to his wife, he suddenly felt love and pity for her, as if only he knew that she had a sickness. He looked over at Dorothy in her thin white hygienist's uniform, her green coat folded over her arm. She had short blond hair and glasses.

The girls had begun to play with a couple of small round dentist's mirrors that Dorothy had brought from Dr. Dressel's office.

Mary Ann, the younger one, brought her mirror close to her eye. "I can't see anything," she said.

"Wait a minute," said Eileen. Her light hair was in half-unraveled braids. Eileen turned her back on Edwin and Dorothy, and positioned her mirror just above her head. "I'm a spy," she said. "Let's see . . . oh, Daddy's putting poison in the mixer." Eileen would say anything.

"I'm a spy, too," said Mary Ann, hurrying to stand beside her sister and waving her mirror. "Show me. Show me how to be a spy."

Edwin couldn't fix Bobbie's mixer and it stayed broken, on a shelf in Edwin and Dorothy's kitchen, for a long time. Meanwhile, Dorothy's working mixer was in the trunk of Edwin's car, and it was a natural thing to pretend it was Bobbie's and take it to her house the next time he visited.

On many Thursdays Edwin told Dorothy a story about New Jersey, then arranged a light day and drove to Brooklyn to visit Bobbie. Bobbie prepared a good dinner that tasted Jewish to Edwin, though she said she wasn't kosher. Little Bradley sat on a telephone book and still his face was an inch off the plate, which he stared at, eating mostly mashed potatoes. "They're better the way Aunt Sylvia makes them, with the mixer," Bobbie said on this particular Thursday, the Thursday on which Edwin had brought her his wife's Sunbeam Mixmaster and pretended it was hers.

"I'm sorry I couldn't bring it sooner, babe."

"Oh, I didn't mean that. I just don't bother, the way Sylvia does."

Edwin watched Bradley. With the mental agility born of his

mixer exchange, Edwin imagined carrying Bradley off in similar fashion and replacing him, just temporarily, with talky Eileen. If her big sister was out of the way, Mary Ann would play with Bradley, while Bobbie would enjoy fussing with a girl.

"What are you thinking about?" said Bobbie.

"I wish I could take Bradley home to meet my mother."

"Take both of us. She won't be against Jewish girls once she sees me," said Bobbie. "I don't mean I'm so special, but I don't do anything strange."

She hurried to clean up and put Bradley to bed, while Edwin, who hadn't replied, watched television. He couldn't help thinking that his family was surely watching the same show, with Groucho Marx. Over the noise of Groucho's voice and the audience's laughter, Edwin heard Bobbie's voice now and then as she read aloud. " 'Faster, faster!' cried the bird," Bobbie read. Soon she came in and Edwin reached for her hand, but she shook her head. She always waited until Bradley was asleep, but that didn't take long. When she checked and returned smiling, Edwin turned off the set and put his hands on her shoulders, then moved them down her back and fumbled with her brassiere through her blouse. Dorothy wore full slips. Edwin pulled Bobbie's ruffled pink blouse free and reached his hand under it. Even using only one hand, he'd learned that if he worked from bottom to top, pushing with one finger and pulling with two others, he could undo all three hooks of her brassiere without seeing them. In a moment his hand was on her big round breast, and she was laughing and opening her mouth for him, already leading him toward her bed.

.   .   .

Edwin forgot that Dorothy had promised Dr. Dressel she'd work Saturday morning. As he dressed in Bobbie's dark bedroom on Thursday night, she asked, "Will you come Saturday?"

"Sure, babe," he said. He had fallen asleep, but he could tell from Bobbie's voice that she'd remained awake, lying naked next to him. He leaned over to kiss her, then let himself out, rubbing his hand on his lips and checking for lipstick stains.

But on Saturday he had to stay with Eileen and Mary Ann, then pick up Dorothy at Dr. Dressel's office. He was more at ease with the girls in the car than at home. Made restless by his broken promise to Bobbie, he left too early, then had to look after his children in the dentist's waiting room. He didn't know how to braid Eileen's hair and it had not been done that morning; Edwin noticed as he reread the dentist's posters, which urged him to eat carrots and apples, that one of yesterday's rubber bands still dangled off Eileen's mussed hair. He called to her and tried to remove the band without pulling. "You're hurting me," she said, though he didn't think he was.

At last Dorothy came out in her coat. "I heard them whooping it up," she said, but she sounded amused. She took two rubber bands from the receptionist's desk and swiftly braided Eileen's hair. Leaving the car where it was, they walked to a nearby luncheonette. Dorothy took Edwin's hand. Sometimes she spoke to him in baby talk; it was a kind of game. "I am going to teach you to bwaid hair," she said. But he didn't know how to answer, so she spoke again, now taking his part, in a gruff voice like the Three

Bears. *"How on earth do you braid hair?"* He let go of her hand and put his arm around her shoulders as she answered with elaborate patience, "Well, first you make a center part. . . ." Edwin imagined Bobbie watching them, not jealously. "Squeeze," the imaginary Bobbie said, and Edwin squeezed his wife's taut shoulder through the green coat.

Bobbie didn't use her mixer often. She was not sufficiently interested in its departure and return to put it away, so she left it on the extra chair next to the kitchen table where Edwin had put it. On Saturday morning she put on makeup and stockings, but he didn't come. Ordinarily, if Edwin didn't appear by a quarter to ten, Bobbie took Bradley out, rather than brooding. This Saturday, though, Bradley had a cold. To distract herself, Bobbie called Sylvia, who asked, "Does he have a temperature?" Bobbie's thermometer was broken, so Sylvia brought hers over. Bobbie made coffee. Bradley sat on the floor in his pajamas, wiping his nose on his sleeve while putting together a jigsaw puzzle, a map of the United States.

Bobbie offered Sylvia a cookie and she and Bradley said together, "Before lunch?" but then everyone took a Mallomar, since Bobbie said a cookie might cheer her up. Bradley licked his fingers and then placed Florida in the puzzle correctly.

"Edwin didn't come today?" Sylvia said, playing with her spoon.

"Sometimes he's busy on Saturdays."

"You need more."

"I manage," Bobbie said. If Sylvia knew all Edwin's ways, she thought, she wouldn't object to him. "He's worth it."

Sylvia laughed, stretching her arm and actually taking a second cookie. "Oh, I know what you mean," she said. She interrupted herself to supervise Bradley's placement of California. "I know what you see in your Edwin. I see the way he looks at you."

"When you've been married a long time," Bobbie said, "I guess it's not so exciting."

Sylvia laughed. "I know how you feel," she said again, not scolding.

"You mean you felt that way about Lou, once."

"Well, I suppose."

"What *did* you mean?" Bobbie said.

"Oh, I shouldn't say anything," Sylvia said. She tipped the bowl of her spoon with one finger, making the handle rise.

"He's not listening," Bobbie said, tilting her head toward Bradley. "You mean—someone?"

"Someone I met at an in-service course."

"Another teacher? A man."

"He teaches at Midwood."

"A high school teacher. You—have feelings?" Bobbie said.

"Did this ever happen to you?" Sylvia said, now glad—it seemed—to talk. "At night, you know, picturing the wrong person?"

Bobbie thought she knew what Sylvia meant. She wasn't sure what an in-service course was, whether it consisted of one occasion or several. "How many times have you seen him?"

"Wait a minute," said Sylvia, but then she crouched on the floor. "Doesn't Colorado belong where you put Wyoming, Bradley?" Wyoming was nice and tight. "Could the map be wrong?"

"Did you have lunch with him?"

"Oh, I'm exaggerating, it's nothing," Sylvia said. She remained on the floor, helping Bradley with a few more states. Then she got up, reaching out a hand to steady herself on the extra chair. She gave the Mixmaster a pat. "Hey, you didn't just buy this, did you?"

"No, I've had it for a while."

"I might have been able to get you a discount. A client of Lou's . . ."

"I bought it last year."

"Oh, right." Sylvia seemed to expect Bobbie to explain why the mixer was on the chair, so Bobbie told in full the story Sylvia had heard only in part: the story of the dress, the walk to the post office, and her return to find Edwin fixing a mixer that wasn't broken.

"He took it home? Why did he do that?" Sylvia asked.

"At home he has tools."

"Maybe he took it to a repair place."

"Oh, no. I'm sure he fixed it himself," said Bobbie.

"You're sure he brought back the same mixer?"

"You mean he bought me a new one? I hope not!" Bobbie said.

"Or he could have bought a used one," said Sylvia.

"Oh, stop being so suspicious." She liked the more tremulous Sylvia who had spoken of the teacher from Midwood High School. She wasn't ready, yet, for the usual Sylvia. "Of course it's mine."

But as she spoke, as she insisted it was hers, Bobbie suddenly sensed that the mixer on the chair might never have been in her house before, and then, looking hard, she was certain. It was the same, but somehow not the same. It had been cleaned differently, maybe with a sponge, not a dishrag. But that thought was ridiculous. It had been handled in a way that was not Jewish. An even more ridiculous thought.

Bradley had abandoned the puzzle and left the room. Maybe Sylvia would say more. "Did you have lunch with him?" Bobbie asked again.

But Sylvia would not be deterred. "Maybe Edwin has another girlfriend," she said, "and this is her mixer. Hey, maybe he has a wife!" She gave a short laugh.

"He has a mother. . . ." said Bobbie. His mother didn't sound like someone who'd plug in a mixer and mix anything. She now remembered that the metal plate with the "Sunbeam" insignia on her mixer was chipped. She looked, and this one was whole. She looked again. "I *trust* Edwin," she said.

"I know you do. Boy, that would be something," Sylvia said. "If it turned out Edwin was married."

But Bobbie was experiencing one of those moments when one discovers the speed of thought by having several in an instant. First she felt ashamed of being stupid. Of course there had been plenty of hints that Edwin was married. Once she allowed herself to consider the possibility, she was sure it was so. Bobbie didn't need to know whose mixer it was to know that Edwin was married. Then, however, Bobbie felt something quite different. It wasn't anger at Sylvia, at her sister's gossipy curiosity.

She was not angry at Sylvia. She felt sorry for Sylvia, a little superior to Sylvia. All her life, Bobbie had known that Sylvia was smart, so Bobbie must be smart, too, even Bobbie who carried her clothing back and forth to the post office. Once they knew Edwin was married, Sylvia would imagine there was only one way to behave—to laugh bitterly—but Bobbie understood that there were two.

That there were two different ways to think about Edwin's marriage—like thinking about the stars, which might be spots of light, close together, and might be distant wild fireworlds—struck Bobbie with almost as much force as her sorrow. Sylvia's way would be to laugh bitterly and tell everyone the story. Edwin's marriage might be a bad joke on Bobbie, but then Edwin would no longer tip his chair against her sink, or walk her to her bed while his hands grasped all of her body he could reach under her loosened clothes. His marriage might be a bitter joke—or it might be something Bobbie just had to put up with.

Bobbie would never marry Edwin, but Bobbie had the mixer that worked. She stood and plugged it in, and it made its noise. The years to come, during which she'd keep Edwin's secret, not letting him know she knew—because it would scare him away—and not letting her sisters know she knew—because they'd scream at her to forget him—became real in her mind, as if she could feel all their length, their loneliness, at once. She would be separated from Edwin, despite Thursday evenings and Saturday mornings. Bobbie turned off the mixer and wept.

"Oh, of course he's not married," Sylvia said, and Bobbie didn't say that wasn't why she was crying. "Me and my big mouth, as usual," Sylvia continued. She stood up and put her arms around Bobbie, and then the sisters were hugging and smiling. "Edwin married," Sylvia said. "If there's one man on earth who couldn't manage being a two-timer, it's Edwin. Sorry, baby, I love the guy, but that swift he's not." And she went on and on, hugging her sister and calling her baby. Baby! The unaccustomed sweetness, like the cookie, comforted Bobbie for a while. Maybe she and Sylvia both had secrets, like Edwin. Maybe life required secrets. What an idea.

Not Yet, Not Yet

Visiting from Boston with her baby, Ruth watched as her father uncapped his fountain pen. On a paper napkin, he drew a map of his Brooklyn neighborhood, where she'd grown up. Her father's large, well-shaped ears stuck out from his bald head, and his chin was pointed, giving him a resemblance to an alert Greek vase. He struck a spot on the map with his finger until it seemed the napkin would shred. But his finger concealed the street Ruth didn't remember—where her sister, "Lillian with all her troubles," now lived. It was 1974. Ruth had graduated from Brooklyn College a decade earlier and immediately moved away.

"So what's your secret?" said her mother. "How come the psychiatrist says she can see *you*?"

"I don't have a secret," said Ruth. In a phone conversation, Lilly had said, "I want to see the baby."

"She's a few blocks away, and we haven't seen her for a year," said Fanny. She imitated Lillian's breathy voice. " 'Not yet,' she says. 'Not yet.' " Fanny left the room.

Ruth's baby was asleep in the bedroom. "Don't wake Laura,"

she called. She'd had lunch with her parents and would spend a couple of hours with her sister. Then she and the baby would stay with a friend in the city and take an early train home in the morning. Her parents, hoping for more, had borrowed a Portacrib.

Her father added streets to his map. When Ruth was a college freshman, she and Lilly had once spent an afternoon in the public library, disputing in whispers the exact *kind* of Greek vase he resembled. Ruth was writing a paper about Greek art. When she noticed that the vases looked like her father, Lilly put aside her homework to help her choose the best likeness from a chart. Daddy was definitely a *kalpis,* Ruth had said, pointing and striking the page as her father did now, years later. His face had the shape of a *kalpis*—round, narrow at the bottom—though the handles on that vase, while they were in the right place, were not shaped like ears.

But her sister had found a picture of a *neck-amphora.* "The ears, the *ears,"* said Lilly, who was babyish, though she was more developed than flat-chested Ruth. Lillian almost wept. The handles of the *neck-amphora* were high, growing (as it were) out of their father's temples—but they were earlike: thin curved strips attached at both ends, exactly like outlines of Daddy's ears.

Lillian's adult troubles did not include protruding ears. Ruth had them, but long hair had concealed them from the time she'd first had the brains to look critically in a mirror, around the time of the paper on Greek art. Now she looked at herself more often than she could bear to as a girl, and as her father continued to work on his map, she stared at her own hands, pressed onto the tabletop, and noticed that her mother's garnet ring was missing from her finger. She suppressed her cry, put her hands in her lap, and glanced behind her, but Fanny had not returned.

At 1:00 A.M. the night before the paper on Greek art was due, Ruth's father had demanded that Ruth stop typing or leave his house. "You mean if I leave I can *keep* typing?" asked Ruth cruelly. They lived in a two-family house, and her father said the family downstairs might be disturbed by the clattering of the old Royal portable. Ruth was a slow typist, especially in those days, before she discovered Corrasable Bond. She erased her frequent mistakes with a pink rubber disk on which a black brush swiveled. With scraps of paper inserted between the first copy and the carbon paper, she protected her carbon copy from smudges, though nobody would ever read it. When her father began to shout, Ruth put down her eraser, got her coat, and left, figuring she'd walk all night, quit college in the morning, and find a job and an apartment. Maybe one of her aunts would take her in. Two of her mother's sisters, Aunt Sylvia and Aunt Bobbie, lived in the neighborhood.

But Ruth's mother had hurried down the stairs behind her. It was a cold night, and Fanny suggested they sit in the car, which was parked in front of the house. After a while she persuaded Ruth to go back upstairs with her. Her father sulked, looking exactly like a *kalpis*, but didn't speak as she finished typing.

Ruth grew her hair after that. "Daddy's ears don't stick out and neither do yours," said Fanny, but Ruth had never been sorry she'd grown her hair. She'd kept it shoulder length when she first had a job, but now she was an editor at the *Boston Phoenix*, where nobody cared if her hair came down to her butt, which it did. Ruth had moved to Boston to live with a man who made her parents nervous, a carpenter named Charlie who had once been a graduate student of philosophy. Now they were married and had two children: David, who was at his co-op day-care center in Brookline, and Laura, asleep in the borrowed Portacrib.

Ruth's father said, "It's a bad idea, going to Lillian's neighborhood."

"It's so different from this neighborhood?"

"Very different. You wouldn't know. I see a little black boy, I can tell if he's just fooling around or he has a knife."

"Oh, for heaven's sake, Dad!" He, a thirties lefty, who used to relish city life, its mixing of races and nationalities!

Ruth's mother returned with Laura against her shoulder, the baby's face hidden in her grandmother's neck. "Here's this sleepy girl." Fanny kissed the origin point of her granddaughter's hair, the center of a light swirl, then kept her nose there.

Ruth also liked the smell of her daughter's scrap of hair, but she said, "Did you wake her?"

"No, I heard her stirring."

"You woke her up!" Ruth glanced at the floor under the table, trying to look for the missing ring without attracting attention.

"She should eat before you go."

Her mother liked watching Ruth breast-feed, though the sight made her explain, each time, why she hadn't nursed Ruth and Lillian.

Her parents weren't old enough to be indulged. They weren't charming and harmless, like the old people on Ruth's street in Brookline. One way or another, they had to be responsible for Lilly's troubles. Ruth dressed the baby, kissed her mother and father, and left, carrying her daughter in one arm while bumping the folded umbrella stroller down the stairs.

"Was it loose?"

"I guess so."

"She should have given it to me," Lilly said. "I have fatter fingers."

"She should have." Their mother had presented the ring to Ruth at a sentimental moment: a third birthday party for David, a boy who loved his grandmother. David had given their mother's powdered and rouged face so many kisses that his own face was smeared and mottled.

"If I find it, will you give it to me?" Lilly said.

Ruth hesitated. Probably she had lost the ring on the subway. There was no way Lilly could find it. Ruth liked the ring. She liked red.

They ordered soup. "We can give some to the baby," Lilly said.

"She doesn't eat solid foods yet," said Ruth.

"Soup is a liquid."

"I mean she eats only breast milk."

"It will be good for her," Lilly persisted. "I remember wanting to eat, and Mom and Daddy refused me all sorts of things." The soup came, brought by a young black waitress, to whom Lilly said, "Well, you don't look Chinese." Laura, beside their table in her stroller, stretched her arms up, so Ruth took her out and held her on her lap. The baby nosed her chest and Ruth tried to get her to face front.

Lilly took a first spoonful of soup, blew on it, and reached across the table, holding it to her niece's lips, but Ruth knocked the spoon out of Lilly's hand, spilling the soup.

"What'd you do that for? A little soup won't hurt her."

"It's hot."

"But I blew." Ruth fumbled with napkins, trembling a little, trying to mop what she'd spilled, which seemed like a great quantity of eggdrop soup for one spoon. The young waitress gave her several more napkins, though Ruth tried to wave her away.

"You won't give me the ring if I find it?" said Lilly.

"Well, what will you give me in exchange?" said Ruth, trying to sound jokey.

"Oh, now I have to think. I could tell you a secret."

"You're always telling me secrets. Secrets are free." Last time they'd met, when Ruth was pregnant, Lilly had told her a long story about a man who refused to make love to her. "He says I'm ugly and bad and I don't deserve his semen," Lilly had said. "Maybe it's true."

Ruth ate her soup, blowing and blowing as if to prove something. It wasn't terribly hot. "Is it true your shrink says you can't see the progenitors?" she said.

"The progenitors. I haven't called them that for a while."

Ruth had used their old word to make friends again, after the soup incident. "Remember when we decided Daddy looked like a Greek vase?" she said.

"Yes . . ." said Lilly tentatively. "Yes! Because of his ears!"

"He still does. We were pretty smart kids, Lilly." She pulled up her sweater and gave her daughter a little more milk. Nursing soothed them both. Then she buckled Laura into the stroller again. "But what was it Mom looked like?"

"Something to do with vases?" Lillian ordered egg rolls and pork fried rice, and persuaded Ruth to have some. The food was good.

"The flowers in the vase," Ruth said, suddenly remembering. "Last week's tulips, we used to say. God, we were mean."

"Do you think your kids will say things like that about you?"

Ruth glanced at Laura, who had turned her head sideways and was noisily sucking the stroller's aluminum support. She said, "I'm trying not to do what Mom and Daddy did." Yet what had their parents done—done to them, done to Lillian? Ruth and Lilly had not been whipped or raped.

Lillian's mind sometimes moved exactly as hers did. "They didn't hit us much," she said.

They paid the check and began walking again. "You'd better tell me what you want in exchange for the ring," Lilly said, after a block.

"Oh, goodness. I want you to see Mom and Dad."

"Not yet."

"Why not? They're old. They're harmless."

"No, they're not."

"What did they do to you? I mean, I know they could be awful. But parents are awful."

"Laura, is she awful?" Lilly said, scooting around in front of the stroller and squatting. She kissed Laura's nose.

"Suppose you promise not to attempt suicide again?" Ruth said then. "You could give me that."

"Not kill myself? I can't promise."

"Whatever they did, Lilly, they don't deserve this. . . ."

"They didn't do much of anything, but somehow I came out of their house thinking I was worthless." She stood, but didn't move, still blocking the stroller. "Do you think it was just built into me?"

"God knows."

"Once Daddy kept track for a whole weekend of how many cookies I ate, and then surprised me with the number. Twenty."

"Not so many." Was that all Lilly could come up with? So

27

many suicide attempts, because of twenty cookies? Ruth angled the stroller around Lilly and they set off again. She knew that wasn't fair.

"Well, he thought so. I thought so."

"I know. And you could go on."

"And I could go on."

"Is it really the shrink's idea?"

"Actually, yes," said Lilly, thrusting her hands in her pockets. "He had to talk me into it. Now and then I burst into tears and say I have to see them. Mom, at least." She brightened. "But what about the ring? What shall I give you?"

Ruth considered. "The only other thing I can ask for is your sofa, but I can't take it home and you wouldn't have any furniture without it."

"No, you can't have Agatha either. Maybe I don't want the ring, if I wouldn't give up anything for it. Oh, I guess I would." She stopped again and faced Ruth. "I'll give you something. I'll give you something you'll be glad to have."

"What?"

"Won't tell."

"But you're not going to find the ring, so I'll never know."

"Oh," said Lilly, "the ring's hanging off the bottom of your sweater."

Hands shaking, Ruth reached under her jacket for the lower edge of the sweater, turning it up as if to keep the ring from falling, though if it hadn't fallen by now . . . but she didn't feel it. "You knew where it was, and you didn't tell me? Now it's gone, Lilly! Should we go back?"

"That girl won't tell us, if she found it."

"That's the sort of prejudiced thing Dad would say."

"Not because she's black, because she's young. I wouldn't have told, at her age."

"You didn't tell now."

"But I might not have gotten it, now."

"Well, I think you won't get it. It's gone." In the street, with the wind blowing, Ruth took off her jacket, handed it to her sister, and found the little gold ring clinging to her sweater, a thread caught in one of the prongs that held the garnet in place.

"So what are you going to give me?" she said then, grasping the ring and remembering how much she liked it, how much better it made her feel about her mother. The baby began to cry.

Lillian fumbled in her coat pocket, still holding Ruth's jacket. She brought out an old camping knife with hinged blades, metal edges—somewhat discolored—and translucent green faces. A gold Girl Scout emblem was visible through the green. Ruth knew she'd once known the knife well. She said, "Where did you get it?"

"It was yours," said Lilly. "Don't you recognize it?"

"How long have you had it?"

"A couple of years. I found it in their junk drawer, on a week-end pass from the hospital."

"That's what you used, those times?"

"That's what I used."

Ruth took the knife and handed over the ring. She was terribly cold. She put on her jacket and buttoned it. Laura was wailing, and Ruth set forth once more, while her sister scurried to catch up. Ruth said, "It was sharp enough?"

"I managed."

Ruth put the knife in her pocket and then reached after it, pushing the stroller with one hand so she could close her other hand around the knife. She had the odd thought that she'd like to put it into her mouth—closed—and run her tongue over the smooth green surfaces and over the dull outside edges of the closed blades. Maybe she used to do that.

"Don't let your kids get near it," said Lilly, and no doubt only meant that children might hurt themselves on something sharp, but Ruth heard her differently. "You mean you think they'll be like you?" she said.

"They'll kill themselves? That's always an option," said Lilly.

Ruth resolved never to see her sister again, never to touch the knife. They had returned to Lilly's house. It was almost time for Ruth to leave for the subway to meet her friend, but she couldn't just leave, her ring gone, the knife in her pocket, Lilly's bitter voice in her head. She went inside, unzipped Laura's snowsuit, and unbuttoned her own jacket. Lilly played Ruth old Judy Collins and Joan Baez records, some that had belonged to both of them, some that Ruth had not known. Laura, awake, sat contentedly in her stroller with the diminishing light from the window behind her. Lilly closed the venetian blinds and turned on an overhead light, then danced to the records. She'd put the garnet ring on her left ring finger.

"You put it on your marriage finger," Ruth said.

Lilly danced for another moment, heavy but graceful, then said, "Well, maybe I'll marry Mom." She clowned a little for Laura, who gazed and then smiled.

Rising to leave, Ruth detoured to the bathroom. As she

washed her hands she heard Lilly's voice, sounding uncertain. She turned off the faucet. "What?"

"She's got the cord—is that all right?" said Lilly nervously as Ruth stepped out of the bathroom. Laura had found the looped cord of the venetian blind dangling next to her stroller—or Lilly had given it to her—and was gumming and sucking it. She was too young, of course, to put it around her neck and tighten it, even if her aunt, who stood stiffly again, arms at her sides, couldn't bring herself to deprive her of it. Ruth picked Laura up and carried her away from the stroller, and now the cord stretched behind the baby as if she were a kite. Ruth unhooked Laura's wet hand from the cord, set her in the stroller, and reached into her pocket for the old Girl Scout knife. She cut the cord in several places.

"But I need it to open my blinds."

"Did you try to strangle yourself, too?"

"Oh, Ruth, not *seriously*. Do you know what I weigh? I'd pull the blinds down, not to mention the molding. That wasn't one of my *real* tries."

Ruth closed the knife and put it back into her pocket, looking at her sister, who had tentatively begun to dance again. She seized Lilly's wide face with both hands. Lilly was taller than she was, and she had to reach up. "Listen to me!" she said, and Lilly stopped swaying and began to cry. Ruth kissed the fat, wet cheek closer to her. "I want you back," Ruth said. Lilly was swaying again.

I Am Not Your Mother

Before they had ever lived in the house, somebody's useless cow had sickened and died in the shed next door. The shaggy rope that tethered her still lay in a corner, so when Sonia figured out that her older sister, Goldie, was having to do with a boy, she got up in the night, disentangled the rope, and tied Goldie to a leg of their bed.

Goldie never sneaked out at night. The town was dark even during the day. Wooden sheds, shops, and houses leaned into one another, creating attenuated triangles of shadow that met and crossed and made further overlapping triangles: layers of deeper shadow. It wasn't hard for Goldie to meet the boy—who was tall and chubby, with a laugh that flung droplets onto her cheeks and made her ears tingle—during what was known as day.

In the morning, Goldie's leg jerked sideways when she turned to put her feet on the floor, and she laughed at her sister's trick, then untied the rope and tied up Sonia, who was still sleeping. The rope's rough fibers had hurt Sonia's fingers. When she felt Goldie's touch on her ankle, in her sleep, her sore hand went to her mouth. Sonia, at fourteen, still sucked her thumb.

Goldie became pregnant. Their parents were frightened. Nothing like this had happened in either of their families before. They hadn't known about the tall boy—who had gone to America. (Everyone wanted to leave if possible.) The parents never spoke of Goldie's big belly, but at last Aunt Leah, the mother's sister, came to see them. "Reuben and I have money for the ship," she said. "Give us the baby." Leah and Reuben had no children. Goldie screamed in childbirth and for days after, bleeding in the bed. The baby, a girl, was taken the day of her birth. Goldie's breasts were hot. They felt as if they were about to explode. "Suck me, suck me," she cried to Sonia at night.

Aunt Leah was religious. She went to the ritual bath; when she married, she'd cut off her hair, and now wore a dusty wig. Goldie cried, "She'll shave my baby's head!" Sonia was impressed that her sister could imagine the bald baby they'd barely seen (whose ineffective kicks and arm-swats Sonia couldn't forget), as a grown girl with hair, getting married. Maybe in New York life would be different, Sonia told Goldie.

Aunt Leah, Uncle Reuben, and the baby, Rebecca (who was theirs, they told people), emigrated promptly. Goldie recovered quickly from childbirth but she looked voluptuous from then on. A man who worked on the roads married her, though Sonia disliked him. He talked loudly in the presence of their still frightened parents, but going to America was easy for him. He couldn't imagine things the rest of them feared, and didn't understand how far away and wide the ocean was. Everyone had letters from relatives about the horrors of the passage, the trials of Ellis Island—but he didn't believe. Goldie, who could read a little, tried to show him a map in a schoolbook, but he tore out the page, saying, "Nothing like that." Sonia couldn't read but had some respect for print. She was shocked, but her angry brother-in-law, whose name was Aaron, was making a point: his experience—simpler than other people's—never did resemble what people who spoke in detail described, not to mention the subtleties reportedly found in books. In a moment he uncrumpled the map. "All right, we'll go to that place," he said, waving at half of North America.

They followed a cousin of his to Chicago. Goldie had mixed feelings. She would never have been permitted to tell Rebecca the truth. Aaron knew about the laughing boy and the baby, but didn't believe in them either. In Chicago, nothing turned out as Goldie expected it to; Aaron's habit of doubt felt reasonable. Hardest was losing her daughter, but now Goldie was also separated from her parents and from Sonia, who couldn't even write a letter. Goldie remembered Sonia's shy mouth on her breasts in the middle of the night, her sister's tongue mastering the unfamiliar technique, her teeth held back but just grazing the nipple, giving relief and a terrible pleasure. When Goldie had a baby boy, the old secret made her laugh and cry when he nursed.

She reared her boy, then three more, with spurts of pleasure at the time of the holidays—which she celebrated primarily with food—or when she'd hear indirectly of her sister. Best of all for Aaron and Goldie was sex, which was excellent, but second best was going out. They went to band concerts and parades, vaudeville and the Yiddish theater, then films. They ate out before anyone they knew. Aaron made a reasonable amount of money, not working on the roads here but selling fruit off a pushcart and later in a store. Goldie sometimes watched her husband when he didn't see her, across the street from his pushcart or outside his store, observing him with a customer. His big mouth opened wide when he spoke, and sometimes she thought she could hear his loud voice—dismissing, denying, doubting—even when she should have been out of earshot.

Sonia married a man who whispered respectfully to her parents. They couldn't always hear him, but they liked him. She soon had a girl and a boy. When her husband, Joseph, left for America alone, he announced his plans in such hushed conferences that nobody was surprised when he did what he said he'd do: he secured a job in New York and after two years sent money for his wife's passage, his children's, and his in-laws'. His own parents were dead. But Sonia's mother had something wrong with her eyes and was afraid she'd be turned back at Ellis Island. Saying good-bye at the train, Sonia and her parents pretended that their only important task was to make sure the children were warm enough. Their grandmother wrapped them in so many shawls, wiping her eyes with the corners, that the children could scarcely move.

On the trip to New York, Sonia thought only of her mother and father, whom she'd never see again. She was afraid she wouldn't find Goldie, and she couldn't remember why she cared about Joseph, but he met her in New York and had not lost his distinctive smell or sound; he had a quizzical way of speaking, as if he found himself a bit foolish, and in turn found that discovery amusing. The babies who were no longer babies made him shake his head in silence. When they were settled, Joseph wrote letters to Goldie for Sonia. The second summer, Goldie and Aaron and—by then—three boys came overnight on the train to visit. Sonia had had another daughter.

One day when Joseph was at work and Aaron was engrossed in a game of pinochle taking place in the street—not shouting for once—the sisters and their children called on Aunt Leah, who lived at the end of a trolley ride. Goldie trembled when Leah's sturdy daughter kissed her gravely. Rebecca took little interest in the cousin from Chicago and her boys, but asked to hold Sonia's baby. Aunt Leah was quiet, and they quickly returned on the trolley to Sonia's house, not talking, busying themselves with the children. The next night, Aaron insisted that the women leave the children with a neighbor, and they all went to a boisterous performance at the theater. The actors' shouts, their stylized and exaggerated gestures, seemed to calm Aaron. Otherwise he was constantly restless; Sonia didn't know what he wanted and that made her feel like a bad hostess. She wondered what it was like to be Aaron, and got far enough to sense his relief when something was vacant, when nothing was inscribed on an object or a moment, so he didn't have to deny whatever others discerned in it.

Rebecca knew Sonia as a cousin, and Sonia's children—the boy, Morris, and, eventually, five sisters (Clara, Fanny, Sylvia, Bobbie, Minnie)—as slightly more distant cousins. At nine, Rebecca scolded Cousin Sonia for insufficient attention to the Passover restrictions, and Sonia spoke sharply, then touched Rebecca's arm apologetically. Rebecca began taking the trolley herself to help Sonia with the children. She took good care of them, but was too strict about keeping them clean and quiet. She had unruly curly hair and a neat little nose rather like Reuben's, not that her father ever looked up from the Talmud to notice her. Cousin Rebecca didn't laugh, Morris and the girls complained. They sat her down and played her their favorite of a pile of records that their father had brought home one night, along with a Victrola: it was called "No News but What Killed the Dog," and told a story Rebecca found sad, though the others shrieked with laughter.

Rebecca finished high school and found a job typing. It was a Jewish company and they gave her Saturday off, or she wouldn't have done it. Sonia's children didn't see her as often once she was working, but sometimes she'd come on Sundays. "Can I help, Cousin Sonia?" Rebecca would say, walking into the preparation of a meal or the bathing of small children. She said it so often that "Can I help, Cousin Sonia?" became a household joke, and the girls said it to one another whenever anybody picked up a dishrag or a paring knife.

Sonia had never learned to read—Sylvia tried to teach her, but Sonia's eyes became red and watery and the project was abandoned—but the children read Goldie's letters out loud to her and she dictated replies. Sonia mentioned Rebecca only occasionally in her letters, not wanting to make her children wonder or make Goldie sad. Rebecca stared when Sonia's girls talked about Aunt Chicago, as they called Goldie: Aunt Chicago ate in restaurants, went to plays, and wrote letters containing sentences about the bedroom.

One day Fanny screamed because she'd read ahead in a letter from Goldie to her mother. Sonia screamed, too, before she even knew what had happened. Aaron had disappeared: one day he had taken his shoes to the shoemaker's for new heels, and had never returned. The shoemaker said he didn't remember Goldie's husband or his shoes, and that was that. Goldie's oldest son had been talking about quitting school and going to work. Now he did so, and Goldie took a job in a dress factory.

Sonia pictured her brother-in-law, in shoes run down at the heel, walking into nothing—finding, at last, some fragment of life where for some reason nobody told him about what he couldn't believe in. "It's a disease," she told her family. "He can't remember where he lives. The police will bring him home when they figure it out."

Goldie wrote, "At last it's quiet around here, but I miss you-know-what."

Joseph sent Goldie money. He had worked in a furniture store for years, and now he was part owner.

Several years after Rebecca graduated from high school, a friend married and quit her job, a *good* job: selling and keeping the books in a store that sold musical instruments and sheet music. The friend told the two bosses (who never yelled, she said) about Rebecca, who was hired after an interview, even though they were not Jewish and she said she wouldn't work on Saturdays. "I understand," said Mr. Hardy, the younger boss, nodding respectfully.

The store was called Stevens and Hardy. Mr. Stevens was an elderly man who could repair any musical instrument, while polite Mr. Hardy, who knew little about music, talked to customers. He was a widower in his forties, with two daughters. The third week Rebecca worked in the store, she was straightening the racks of music in the evening, after Mr. Stevens had left and they'd closed, when she was suddenly gripped around the legs. She looked down, alarmed. A little girl whose hair needed combing had seized Rebecca's skirt and was hiding her face in it.

"What's wrong?" Rebecca said.

"Mama died." Mama had not just died, but that was what was wrong. The little girl, Mr. Hardy's younger daughter, Charlotte, was playing a private game with Rebecca or her skirt. At the moment she was not grieving. Nonetheless, Rebecca bent compassionately and touched the child's hair, figuring out who she was.

A tall woman appeared. "I'm sorry, miss," she said. "Charlotte, get up."

Charlotte stayed where she was. The woman was Mr. Hardy's sister. She and Rebecca spoke politely, and then Mr. Hardy came out and introduced them.

The girl still knelt at Rebecca's feet, still with Rebecca's hand on her hair. Facing the child's father and aunt—two well-dressed, blond, self-confident Americans, descendants of George Washington for all Rebecca knew—Rebecca felt for a moment like a participant in an unfamiliar religious rite such as she imagined took place at a church she passed (all but averting her eyes) on her way to work.

"Get up, Charlotte," said Mr. Hardy. Charlotte stood at last, flushed and laughing, and Rebecca's feeling passed. Rebecca swept the floor while Mr. Hardy replaced the trumpets and saxophones that customers had examined in the course of the day, and rechecked lists he'd made, as he did every night—sitting in his tiny office with the door open, singing jazz melodies extremely softly and slowly. When everyone left that evening, Mr. Hardy's sister and Charlotte went out first. Mr. Hardy held the door for Rebecca so as to lock it behind her, and he turned and looked at her in a way that seemed expectant. "Your daughter is pretty," Rebecca said.

Mr. Hardy's cheeks reddened, and then—standing in his coat, holding his hat at his side—he changed suddenly. He seemed to grow slightly shorter and wider; his limbs seemed rounder. It was as if a clever mechanical model of a human being had been replaced by a live person, inevitably less precisely assembled. Mr. Hardy was a gentile, but when he grasped the brass doorknob, Rebecca realized, it felt round and hard to him, exactly as it did to her. She suddenly pictured his arm, under his coat and shirt, full of tangled veins. "How did your wife die, Mr. Hardy?" Rebecca said. "If it's all right to ask."

"It's all right," he said. "She had a ruptured appendix."

"I'm sorry."

"Thank you."

A few weeks later, after Rebecca had found herself having occasional strange thoughts about Mr. Hardy—not just about the veins on his arm but other parts of his body—he invited her to come for a walk. It was spring, and still light when they closed the store. They walked to a German bakery where they drank tea and ate coffee cake. Rebecca, who brought her lunch in a bag, didn't object. The bakery wasn't kosher, but Mr. Hardy was such a conscientious person that she knew he didn't understand and she didn't want to make him feel bad. The walk was repeated.

Her parents didn't ask why Rebecca came home from work later and less hungry. Everything about the music store baffled them; there was no point in inquiring. But Rebecca was surprised at how readily she ate at the bakery, just because poor Mr. Hardy was a widower, a man to be pitied—as if the kosher laws had an exception for tea with the grieving. She asked him questions about his daughters, about his own life. Rebecca was well be-haved, but not shy. At last, on a day when she was particularly en-joying Mr. Hardy, enjoying the look of his neck coming out of his shirt collar, she blurted out, "I'm not supposed to eat at a place like this."

"Even though it's not pork?"

"Yes."

"Your parents mind? Why didn't you tell me?"

"They don't know."

Timothy Hardy was not accustomed to concealing his behav-ior or feeling ashamed of it. He'd assumed she understood he was courting her, and that her parents would, too. Before asking Re-becca to walk, he'd decided he probably would marry her. He planned to give up pork and to accompany her to the Jewish church on Saturdays. He thought her parents would be doubtful at first—he was not Jewish, he had been married, he had children—but they would be reassured when they realized what an upright and serious-minded son-in-law he'd be.

Rebecca had liked Timothy Hardy's seriousness from the start. He reminded her a little of Cousin Sonia's husband, Joseph, who'd parcel out a small chicken with scrupulous fairness to his many children, making ironic, self-deprecating comments, sometimes inaudible except for their tone. Timothy Hardy was not ironic. Irony alarmed him because he couldn't endure the risk of being misunderstood, yet Rebecca had misunderstood him completely. She had not guessed he wanted to marry her. Rebecca didn't know gentiles could marry Jews.

"Tell them," Timothy Hardy now began to urge her, though he still didn't mention marriage. "Tell your mother I've asked you to drink tea. Let me visit her."

"What will you talk about?"

"I'll tell her I'd like to take you to a concert. She'll see that I'm not young, but that isn't so bad."

"I don't think I can do that," said Rebecca. She tried to imagine her mother, who was engaged these weeks in embroidering a Torah cover for the shul, putting down her work and rising to greet Timothy Hardy. It wasn't just that Leah would object to him. She would be as alarmed by his interest in her daughter as if Rebecca reported that the streetcar or the lamppost on the corner wanted to visit her at home.

Mr. Hardy stopped asking her to take walks. He'd spoken of his mother, now dead, with a warmth Rebecca envied, and she knew he wouldn't allow himself to lead a young person into disobedience to her parents. "Whenever I went to see my mother," Timothy had confided one afternoon, "she'd insist she had known just when I'd get there. At last I went to visit her at six in the morning, and she said, 'Well, Timothy, I am surprised to see you!'" After that story he blinked several times, smiling hard, his dimples showing and his mustache looking stretched. Rebecca understood how daring—how loving—it had been for him to go so far as to play a trick.

After taking some walks by herself in a different direction, Rebecca knew that she loved Timothy Hardy, and that he'd given her up because she was too cowardly to tell her mother about him. If she was in love, she thought she ought to be brave enough to tell Leah, even though she was now sure that Timothy Hardy would never take her for a walk or to a concert or anywhere. When she looked at her broad face in the mirror, with heavy curls falling over her forehead—the alert face of someone about to follow instructions carefully—she was astonished to discover that it could be the face of someone in love. She thought she'd like to die saving the lives of Timothy Hardy's children.

One evening, Leah was alone, embroidering near the window, when Rebecca came back from visiting her cousins. The day was fading and it was time to stop and light the lamp, but Leah had kept working, making neat silvery lines and loops, soothed and enchanted by her own skill. When Rebecca came in Leah smiled apologetically. "I should have more light," she acknowledged. Leah's eyesight wasn't as good as it had been.

It was unusual for Leah to sound apologetic or tentative. She was a firm, vigorous person who followed the elaborate dictates of her religion precisely, picturing herself as a small but muscular horse pulling a sledge. Leah had had a deeply pious father and now she had a deeply pious husband. She was grateful to both of them, feeling obscurely that if they hadn't taught her to be quite so scrupulous, something bad would have been freed in her. Her father and husband didn't seem to experience something Leah had known from childhood, a slightly exhilarating, slightly nauseating awareness that truths might also be false. Sometimes a compelling, hateful picture appeared uncontrollably in Leah's mind: the embroidered Torah cover, for example, smeared with feces. Leah knew to keep her head down when that happened, whisper a prayer, and keep embroidering. She'd brought up her daughter carefully.

Rebecca lit the lamp. Her mother looked up and smiled, and Rebecca thought that Leah looked surprisingly young at that moment, with her double chin and the bags under her eyes momentarily in shadow. A look of query passed over Leah's face, and it was almost as if she'd invited her daughter's confidence, and so Rebecca, still in her coat, slid into a chair, rather than seating herself properly, and said, "Mama, I think I love Mr. Hardy."

"I think" was a lie, Rebecca's bow to convention, her effort to sound as she thought she should. She had always been so good that she'd had no practice speaking of hard subjects. Everything she'd said up to now had been something she knew her parents wanted to hear.

Leah looked up, so startled she thought for an instant that she must have imagined rather than heard her daughter's words, and her hand went to her mouth. "Sha!" she said involuntarily, though nobody could hear them.

"But I do."

Rebecca suddenly grinned at her mother like a baby, and her wide face glowed. Leah's hands prickled. She saw herself sitting in her chair, the Torah cover in her lap, as if she were someone else: she had a sensation of disconnection from herself, which she'd had only once before, when someone told her that her father was dead. She said, "He won't . . ."

"He did. I think he's changed his mind, so there's nothing to worry about, but I want to tell him I love him, just so he'll know. He's a good man, Mama. Sometimes when we walk together, he says just what I'm thinking. It's as if he's Jewish."

"Shhh." Leah shook her head hard. It was beyond consideration. They would have to hold a funeral. "You must stop talking like this." It was her fault. Leah should have thought about men. She should have pointed Rebecca toward a man at shul, or spoken to a friend. In Europe it would have been simple. "Rebecca," she said, "would you bring me a glass of water?"

Rebecca hurried out, still in her coat, and brought it, stretching her arm and the glass of water toward her mother when she was still halfway across the room. Leah started to rise and accept the glass, but its surface was slippery, or Rebecca, with new recklessness, let go too soon. The glass did not fall for a moment. Somehow it seemed to rise, and the water—Rebecca had filled it too full—rose in a circle, as well, as if a heavy fish had dived, making a wave that broke over the hands and arms of Rebecca and her mother, and the Torah cover that was still in Leah's other hand. For a moment the water resembled feeling, pure and intense. Then it was just water, and the conversation ended with mopping, broken glass, apologies, and consultations about damp embroidery.

Just after the front door of the store had been locked the next evening, Rebecca stood in front of Timothy Hardy's desk as if she wanted to request permission to buy ink for the ledger. He looked at her over the rims of his glasses. "I would like to tell you that I love you," said Rebecca. "I know you don't want to take me walking anymore, and of course we couldn't . . . I told my mother—"

Timothy sprang up, letting his glasses fall to the desk and slide onto the floor. He seized her by the shoulders. "Marry me," he said. "I will become a Jew."

"You can't."

"I mean I'll convert."

"I don't think . . ."

"Your mother will change her mind when I convert."

She shook her head tearfully. He kissed her.

Timothy went to a synagogue he'd noticed on the Lower East Side. He knew enough to go on Saturday, but he couldn't read the Hebrew information saying what time the service began. He thought 10:00 A.M. would be fine, and when he arrived he saw men coming out and going in, so he walked in behind them and sat down. All around him, men were swaying and murmuring, stopping to converse, swaying and murmuring again. Eventually the scrolls in their silk cover were brought out and Timothy was amazed to see something lavish and colorful in this drab setting. The service went on for hours. When it was over, Timothy approached the rabbi, hat in hand. "Excuse me," he said, "I would like to become Jewish." He wondered if the rabbi spoke English.

"Put on your hat," the rabbi said, and Timothy took that as a dismissal, apologized, and left. Maybe he could find a different synagogue.

Rebecca noticed that her mother looked frightened for weeks after their conversation, and she worried that she'd damaged Leah's health with her surprising admission. She didn't mention Mr. Hardy again. When they were alone in the store, she and Timothy planned their life. She couldn't resist these conversations. She would care for his children, and they'd have more. "Maybe you'd better come see the furniture," he said. "You might not like Lucy's taste." Lucy was his dead wife.

"We're keeping Lucy's furniture," said Rebecca, sounding like her mother.

"You are the bride."

"Bride shmide." She'd found her true work and wanted to get busy. She'd learn to laugh so Timothy and his daughters could laugh. Her cousins could teach her jokes. She'd get them to explain what was so funny about that record "No News but What Killed the Dog," which consisted of a recital of disasters.

One evening Timothy told her that the rabbi who was preparing him to become Jewish, after discouraging him several times, had explained an unexpected next step. It was necessary for Timothy to be circumcised. He looked at Rebecca with love and some embarrassment, and she slowly took in what he was saying. Rebecca had allowed herself, for a few seconds at a time, alone in her bed, to consider that Timothy had a penis, but now it was as if lights had been turned on in a room that should be dark. Staring into Timothy's face, Rebecca acquired a rapid education. Her father must have a penis, too, as well as Cousin Joseph and his son, Morris. When they were little Jewish babies, their little penises had been cut. She had been to a bris more than once. She knew all about mohels and what they do, but she had never allowed herself to think the thoughts she thought now, that baby boys grew into men, that their penises grew, too, that men who were not Jewish had different penises, that a different penis hung at this moment in Timothy's trousers. Involuntarily she glanced down, and then she glanced down frankly. "It will hurt."

"They do something . . ."

"When are you going to do it?"

"Next week. There's a man who does it."

"A mohel."

"Yes."

There would be a sharp knife, slender and very bright. "Shall I come with you?"

"If you would walk to the building with me . . ."

"And wait?"

He hesitated. It was late fall, and Timothy was wearing thick trousers. He stood firmly on his two big legs, which he tended to separate a little. His tweed jacket was thick, too. It seemed to her that his clothing was fur; he was naked in the way an animal is. Rebecca knew she wanted to do something, but at first she didn't know what. Then she pulled her broadcloth blouse free of her skirt. As she pushed it up toward her neck, she knew the gesture was clumsy, that she must look more foolish than alluring, with crushed cloth bunched under her chin. Holding the sturdy material in place, she tried to push aside her slip, which came up high on her chest, with a brassiere under it. Rebecca's breasts were large, and she wore underwear with good support. She took Timothy's hand, which trembled, and drew it under her clothes. He pushed the cloth aside, leaned over her, found and released her breast, and put his mouth on it. He seemed to be crying. "Walk there with me, but then go away," he said.

"But won't you need someone, later?" Her voice had a sob in it, because of the pleasure of his touch on her breast.

"Jews are used to trouble," Timothy said. He was making a joke, the second of his life.

She loved his joke. "Are you really Jewish?" she said.

He stepped back from her and held out his hands, turning them as if the answer was written on them, maybe on his palms, maybe on the backs of his hands. "Shema Yisrael . . ." he began, and though the vowels were flat, Rebecca recognized what he was saying. Her cheeks grew warm, and she straightened her clothes.

All night—shamed, throbbing—Timothy was enraged with himself and with all Jews. He wondered if a cruel trick had been played on him, and if years from now he might discover that circumcision was rare among Jews, and that the rabbi had put him through such an experience as punishment for desiring one of their women. First his wife had died, and now, when he had miraculously fallen in love again, this hideously ludicrous requirement had been placed upon him. A religion that required him to expose himself, that required blood and pain . . . They gave him whiskey, but it just caused a headache. In bed, he tried not to think of his view of the knife, just before the job had been done, despite the mohel's courteous effort to place his black-clothed self between Timothy and the table where it lay. Now his penis felt as large as a melon. If it were infected, he would die and be buried a Jew, to the consternation of his Protestant relatives. Timothy began to pray in Hebrew. Then he prayed in English, to Jesus, the Jew he'd betrayed. As the pain lessened a little, as he began to think he might want to touch his penis to someone else's body again, he imagined the future, in which he and Rebecca would endure derision and shame. Timothy and Rebecca, the well behaved. That was what they had in common, good behavior and the discovery that it meant nothing: it originated in no excellence, afforded no ease or safety.

Timothy wanted to be present when Rebecca told her parents that he had become a Jew, but she refused. Three days after his conversion, she helped her mother cook supper, though her hands shook and she dropped the potatoes. "Stir," Leah said, and Rebecca stirred the soup and skimmed the fat. It was Shabbas. Rebecca waited until her father came into the dining room, then until her mother had spoken the blessing and lit the candles. She still couldn't speak. Once she did, there would be no more eating, and there was no reason to waste the food and leave everyone hungry.

When the plates were almost empty, she put down her fork. "Mama, Papa, I have to tell you something," she said.

Her mother drew her hand to her mouth so abruptly that Rebecca knew she had thought incessantly of their last conversation. Rebecca said, "Mr. Hardy wants to marry me." Her father sat back quickly; obviously Leah hadn't told him. "He has become a Jew," Rebecca continued. Then she started to cry. "Because he loves me. He . . . he went to the mohel. He was cut."

Her father stared. "You didn't tell me?" he said. "Rebecca?"

It hadn't occurred to her how he'd feel. He didn't look angry, as she had expected. He pushed his chair back, looking pinched and fearful, as if he'd been exiled. She'd never seen her father look that way.

Leah had kept her hand on her mouth and now she bit it and pulled it away quickly and then put it on the table. Rebecca could see tooth marks. "Rebecca," said Leah quietly, her voice unsteady, "I am not your mother."

In a rush, Rebecca heard the mumbled story of Goldie the difficult and shameless, who she thought must somehow remind Leah of Timothy—but that wasn't the point. It became clear why Papa, by now, was backing his chair toward the window. The knob at the top of the chair made a star-crack in the glass that nobody noticed until next morning, by which time Rebecca, who'd cried all night, no longer thought of it as her window, or in any sense her responsibility. Yet felt for the poor broken pane a nostalgia that made her weep some more. For calamity had not made Leah's speech extravagant and hyperbolical. Leah was not Rebecca's mother.

She was not Rebecca's mother, Reuben was not her father, but they loved her like parents. They didn't hold a funeral because Rebecca wasn't their daughter and, by means of some chicanery, she was not marrying a gentile. Leah continued embroidering Torah covers and following the laws, but sitting in her chair in the late afternoons, she felt as if the sides of her house had fallen away from the roof, that the furniture around her had slid down slides made by the fallen walls, that the wind blew on her without obstacle.

Sonia's children were amazed, full of whooping and obstreperousness. Rebecca was their first cousin and Sonia, who seemed incapable of secrecy but had known all along, was Rebecca's aunt. After the first hard night, Rebecca had taken the trolley, Shabbas or not, to her cousins' house. "Mama says she's not my mama."

Sonia started and sucked in her breath. "Aunt Chicago is your mama."

Nobody remembered Goldie very well. "Aunt Chicago whose husband walked out."

"That Aaron, the rat."

Five years earlier, when Aaron had left, Rebecca had been dismayed to think of a cousin who couldn't keep track of her husband. "She wasn't married when she had me?"

"She was a girl. What did she know?"

Rebecca got on a bus and went to Chicago, where she located her mother in a tenement that seemed from the outside much like the one where she'd grown up, but was different inside. Rebecca had not thought to telephone Goldie; she'd simply taken the address from Sonia, packed a bag, had a tearful, stubborn conversation at the store with Timothy, and set forth. When Aunt Chicago—who had long gray-brown hair that she hadn't yet braided that morning—opened the door in her bathrobe, a dog pressed past her, wagging her tail and barking. Goldie and Rebecca looked at each other, listening to the dog. Finally Goldie said, "Who?"

"Rebecca."

"From Aunt Leah?"

"She told me."

"They wouldn't let me say anything," said Goldie, before she began to scream so loudly that the neighbors, not knowing whether they heard joy or anguish, came running. Suddenly Rebecca belonged to twenty people and a dog she had never known about: half brothers, friends. The rejoicing involved food, dancing, drink, talk, shouts. Goldie said, "I lost that worthless Aaron but I got my baby back." When Rebecca told her about Timothy, Goldie asked, "What if he can't still do it, from the cutting?"

"It's healing."

"Thank God."

Goldie and the boys needed her as much as Timothy and his girls, but nobody could imagine moving. Changing a religion was one thing, leaving New York or Chicago something else. Rebecca and Goldie wrote letters from then on, and shouted on the telephone. When Aaron had been gone seven years, Goldie had him declared dead. She married a widowed neighbor, a man who was gentle with her. In the end everyone moved to Florida and ran in and out of one another's apartments, but that wasn't until the fifties or sixties, when they began to grow old. Goldie had been so young when Rebecca was born that they grew old together. Timothy was the oldest, but he outlived them all, weeping and praying in a Florida synagogue in his old age, when he looked more Jewish. People asked him what his name was changed from. He thanked God for the happiness he'd had in his life. He and Rebecca, Goldie and her second husband, would all go dancing at a big hotel in Miami Beach. Rebecca always looked like a demure young girl, even as she grew gray, but she learned lightheartedness. At the wedding of one of Goldie's sons, she walked to the microphone in a slinky green satin dress and wished her half brother "every kind of happiness, including with no clothes on." It was Rebecca's closest approximation to a dirty joke. But nothing Rebecca did could be dirty, Timothy thought, remembering—as he drove a big white convertible to the synagogue in the Florida sun—the way she had offered him her breast that first time, drawing his hand under her clothes. How happy he'd been, then and later, bending his head and pressing it into her neck, putting his mouth on Rebecca's breasts.

In the Dark, Who Pats the Air

Jo stood at the foot of the bed in her jeans and sweater, looking at naked Josh, who'd been her roommate for a year and her lover for three months. Josh was solid, small, and fair, with glowing orange hair on his chest and groin. Jo had long black hair. "You're a marmalade cat," she said.

They were about to make love, but they hadn't said so. She waited, as she'd waited all those chaste months, for either to speak or act; she'd known early that they would be lovers.

Josh said, "A Jewish marmalade cat!" Jo was not Jewish. She was Korean-American.

She undressed and lay down. Not touching, they were silent. His penis was erect.

"I'll give you . . ." Josh said then, elongating his words as if he didn't know how he'd finish, "a kiss! And you give me a kiss." They kissed lustily, their tongues busy.

When Jo spoke, to propose her own swaps, her voice was that of a child dressed as a robber. For what if he said no? "I'll give you a bite, you give me a pinch." She bit his shoulder and he pinched her ass. How had they begun this game? Not by discussion or decision. It embarrassed Jo, not because it was kinky; maybe because it wasn't.

Sometimes they made mistakes, they became distracted, and nothing happened. A few days earlier, she'd said, "I'll give you a clothesline, you give me a kiss."

"A *clothesline*?" said Josh.

"Yeah."

"Laundry?"

She was already sorry she'd said it. After a while he said, "Oh, you mean tying me up. Or whipping me. Which?"

"Never *mind*," she said. She'd thought of tying him up, but hadn't intended to go out to their small, square backyard and retrieve an old clothesline she'd noticed.

This time they were not distracted. As she dressed, afterward, she decided that the person who had strung the clothesline, which sagged from a fence to a hook near the back door, was a long-dead Irish woman. The woman had stood on a tottering kitchen chair, wearing an apron. Or she'd awakened her husband—a policeman, possibly, who worked nights—and made him string up the clothesline. The woman talked to him even when he wasn't home, even after he was killed. She was still talking: the apartment was haunted. Jo heard mocking, anguished whispers, occasionally in rudimentary Korean—she was the child of immigrants, and knew a few words—yet the ghost was surely not Jo's dead grandmother, not Korean at all. Surely it was the woman she'd just imagined, thinking all around the clothesline like someone lost in the dark, who pats the air. Had the woman killed her husband? Or was he murdered, and then the murderer came for her, too? She and Josh were being watched: How dare you not be dead? How dare you not be in danger? Jo had gone to Harvard, Josh to Brandeis. Somerville, where both had moved after graduation, had narrow, treeless streets, steep hills, and tiny backyards behind tiny plain, crowded houses. Students and college graduates were taking over old neighborhoods: the air itself sometimes seemed angry.

Jo was a teacher in a day-care center. At work next day she stretched on a rug telling her three-year-olds a story, making it up as she went along. "So Dinah said to the giant, 'I can't reach your hand, or I'd give you a cookie.'" The real Dinah smiled, sweet and untidy in oversized overalls because she'd wet her pants and had to be dressed from the Extras Drawer. "Then Henry"—as Jo nodded to the real Henry—"climbed on Dinah's shoulders. But they were still too small. So they called Krishna."

Krishna was a tiny, serious child who could read.

"'Krishna! Krishna!' they called."

Jo noticed within herself a gray and purple emotion—a Josh-and-sex emotion—instead of her usual primary-color work feeling. As she invented the story of the giant, she stared at a shelf, and on it was another clothesline, knotted every foot and a half. On walks, each child grasped a knot. After the giant finally ate her cookie, Jo brought down the rope and led an indoor jungle walk, past swamps and crocodiles. She liked her job, but when she looked at her watch it was never as late as she'd thought. Neither she nor Josh—who did computer support at a nonprofit—knew what they'd become.

At the end of the day it was Jo's turn to wait with a few children, some from each room, whose parents paid extra to pick them up late. "Sing the train song," the older ones begged. The song was supposed to be about a peanut waiting for a train, but one day she'd used their names, and now they demanded it. She sang:

A Tammy sat on a railroad track,
Her heart was all aflutter.
Around the bend came Engine Ten,
Uh-oh, Tammy butter.

A Krishna sat on a railroad track,
His heart was all aflutter. . . .

She sang with embarrassed gusto as the first parent arrived. Then others came, they greeted their children and one another, they slowly departed—the children subtly different in their parents' presence—and at last the workday was complete.

In welcome silence, Jo coiled the rope. She vacuumed the blue carpet. When she turned off the machine, she heard a knock that was repeated. She opened the street door and a man entered. Had he come to retrieve his child, whom she'd somehow misplaced? "Yes?" she said quickly.

"I'm interested in enrolling my daughter," said the man. He was older than most of the fathers, maybe a professor or a lawyer on his second marriage. He was boyish, in a baseball jacket, but gray-haired.

"Oh! Well, I'm not the right person to talk to. The director's gone."

"May I look around?"

"This is the three-year-old room," said Jo.

"Are you a teacher?" The man sat down on one of the children's chairs.

Now she was annoyed. He was probably thinking, *A Chinese girl.* She said, "There's not much I can tell you. . . . Did you want to start in the summer?"

"She's two," he said.

"When will she be three?"

The man hesitated, and suddenly Jo felt afraid. Then, sure enough, he said, "Do you see this?" He stretched out his hand.

"I have to leave," said Jo.

The man stood, keeping his hand steady as if it held a naturalist's treasure, a leaf or a striated rock. Jo saw what it contained: a small outdoorsman's knife with a black plastic handle.

"It's quite sharp," said the man. "Please take off your clothes."

"What if I don't?" Jo said.

"Please do." He sat down.

So she did, nauseated and longing only for a moment, any moment, after this incident, when she could remember it instead of being in it. For two periods of a few seconds each, she couldn't see the man, as she pulled first her sweater and then her shirt over her head. He said nothing, sitting without moving, the knife still in the palm of his hand, which was held out like an offering. He looked frightened. Sitting on the floor to take off her shoes, she thought of helping the children with their shoes, then of the man's daughter.

"Socks," said the man. She stood to take off her jeans, and undid her bra. Finally she took off her panties, then swiftly sat down on the rough carpet, raised her knees, and hugged them. She made herself look again at the man and he looked back. He stood, put the knife in his pocket, walked to the door, flipped the light switch, and stepped outside, letting the door close behind him and leaving Jo in the dark.

When Jo was late, Josh imagined that a parent had failed to show up, abandoning a child. Finally, Jo would arrive, carrying a damp toddler whom they'd keep—at least overnight. He'd play with it, sitting on the floor, while Jo went to the drugstore for diapers. When Jo came in, he looked up from his computer.

"Did you cook?" Jo said. Her voice sounded odd.

"I lost track of the time," said Josh untruthfully.

"I'm so hungry," said Jo, and began to cry. She opened her bag and took something out—a pair of panties.

"What happened?" said Josh, standing and reaching for her.

Jo shook her head, and went into the bedroom.

"What *happened*?" he said again, when she came out.

"A man——"

"In the street? Somebody raped you?"

She told the story quickly. "He didn't touch me."

"Oh, Jo." He reached to hold her, but didn't feel allowed, and only touched the fuzz above the surface of her sleeve, as he used to do before they were lovers. "Shall I call the cops?"

"I already did. I called Sue and the cops." Sue was the director. Jo hadn't called him, Josh noted. "Could you get some food? I'm so hungry!" she said then. He rushed for the phone book and ordered from an Italian restaurant that delivered; he set the table. He asked questions, which she answered.

"Do you want a drink?" It was what one said.

"Do we have anything?"

They had beer and a bottle of bourbon someone had left there. He poured some bourbon for each of them. Jo added water to hers. "This is good," she said.

"He had a knife?" Josh asked for the second time.

"He had a knife."

"A young kid?"

"No, middle-aged. White. He looked like my comp lit professor."

The doorbell rang and she jumped. "The food," he said apologetically.

Then, as they ate, the phone rang. "Don't answer," said Jo. The caller didn't leave a message. A minute later it rang again, and this time, to Josh's relief, Jo answered. "Hi, Laura," she said. Laura was Josh's second cousin. He'd seen her only a few times as a child, but they'd become friends at Brandeis. Jo hadn't met Laura or talked to her before, but she didn't hand Josh the phone, though he stretched out his arm. From across the room, he could hear Laura's voice chiming up and down in Washington, D.C. His cousin in her ignorance was being cheerful after Jo's bad experience, compounding his own awkwardness.

Then Jo put her hand over the mouthpiece. "She wants to stay here Friday night."

"Do you mind?" Josh said.

She shrugged. They had room, now that Jo had at last moved out of the supposedly haunted back bedroom and into his. They'd gone out for a beer on a Friday night and talked late. As they walked home, he took her hand. "Do you feel strongly that roommates should keep things platonic?" he'd said as they entered the apartment. His hand was almost trembling in hers. He let go to find his key.

"No," Jo had said. "No, I don't, as it happens." Once inside the apartment, she had reached for his hand again.

Now he began clearing the food. Laura, who worked for a congresswoman, had grown up in Boston, but her parents, divorced, lived elsewhere. Josh was flattered that when Laura came to Boston, she wanted to stay with him.

Jo and Laura continued talking. To Josh's surprise, Jo told Laura the whole story in more detail than he'd heard it. She stood and turned, stretching the curly cord around her elbow and then revolving slowly as she spoke, until it was released. She listened, talked, listened. "No, no," she said once, her voice urgent. She leaned forward, and her hair fell forward; then she tipped her head back to clear her face, then leaned forward again. "It wasn't precisely shame," she said. She laughed bitterly. "In the nudity department, it didn't exactly count."

After a pause she said, "Fear of getting killed." Soon she hung up. "They're coming on Friday in time for supper, which they're going to bring."

"They?"

"Her boyfriend. Chandler?"

"I didn't know Laura had a boyfriend."

The director had urged Jo to stay home the day after the assault, but Jo felt uncompromisingly competent, and arrived at work on time. The other teachers knew what had happened; all day, gusts of concern passed to her through walls, or as doors closed. Each adult seemed surrounded by a swirling windstorm of pain. Ignoring them, Jo read picture books to her charges in a loud voice, one book five times.

But at night she was immobile in front of the television, not knowing if she wanted Josh to speak to her or not. "I'll give you . . ." he said, finally, coming to stand behind her. She was watching an old movie. He stood watching behind her, one hand on her shoulder, but didn't speak again.

"No," she said. The movie was a crime story in black and white, set in Scotland, with looming stone fireplaces and sooty pots. A mute child was the only witness to her mother's murder.

"Is she too traumatized to talk?" Josh said, after a while.

"She never talked."

"Where's her father?"

"No father. The girl had a signal, and the mother cut her a piece of bread. Then the mother went out of the room and died, while the girl watched through the window."

"She'll talk," Josh said.

He annoyed her. She turned off the TV, went to bed, and pulled the blankets around her.

In the morning, Josh said, "I dreamed that movie. In my dream, the mother came back to life." Like the mother before she was murdered, he was cutting bread. He liked bread from the bakery, not the supermarket.

"That's sillier than the real movie," Jo said.

"She was under a pile of wood and the child pointed. Then

somebody pulled the wood off. I remember long golden planks lying across the mother, and how she stared up at me."

"*You* pulled the wood off?"

"I guess I was in the movie."

In the movie, the mother had been stabbed with the bread knife, not buried under planks. Josh's bread knife looked nothing like the knife of the man who had assaulted Jo, but Jo found herself angry with Josh for owning and using a knife, for being a snob about packaged, sliced bread. She ate cold cereal.

"Since I moved into your room, I don't dream," Jo said. "The ghost stayed in the back room."

"Now the multitalented ghost causes dreams."

"You don't believe me, but you never slept in there." Jo prided herself on her coolheadedness. The ghost (if that was the right word) was a breath of pessimism, of dread; it could always be sensed in particular parts of the apartment, never in others. The ghost was evidence of her resistance to sentiment, not the opposite. "The ghost was a murderer," she said. "Or she was murdered."

He looked away. "Once you said the ghost was in here," he said. The knife was in his hand. His orange curls hadn't yet been brushed.

"No I didn't." Not in the healthy kitchen. She brought in a notebook and drew a map of the apartment. With dots, she outlined the haunted area. She knew just where her feelings changed.

"The bathroom is closer to the kitchen," Josh said. He took her pen and corrected the drawing.

"That's not precisely my point, is it?" Jo said.

. . .

Friday night Josh hurried to meet Laura's train at South Station. She jumped into his arms. Chandler was hairy. He and Josh grunted and nodded: Greetings, fellow primate. Josh instantly disliked Chandler for daring to sleep with his cousin, who rumpled Josh's curls and said, "You look great!" She handed him a colorful stuffed tote bag, and they took the Red Line to Davis Square. As they climbed Somerville's narrow streets she said she and Chandler had met at a party three months earlier.

"And you're already calling him your boyfriend?" Josh said. "Jo and I didn't even shake hands for a year."

"Impressive technique," said Chandler from behind them. He spoke in a rich voice that was a little too loud. "How did you get her to shake hands after only a year?"

At the apartment Chandler shook hands with Jo and the other two laughed. Josh stepped forward and also shook hands with Jo, and she nodded as if that happened all the time. Jo was a little stern, quiet compared to Laura, who knocked into objects, which quivered behind her but were not harmed. She was short, with wild, light-colored hair something like Josh's. Leading the way into the kitchen, Laura announced that she'd learned to cook Ethiopian food. She'd frozen an entire meal and had let it thaw on the train. She took packages wrapped in foil and plastic from the tote bag. "People began sniffing as we left New York," she said, grabbing her hair as if she'd lost something in it. She'd made injera—the flat sourdough bread—and two kinds of stew.

While Josh and Jo heated the food, Laura phoned an old roommate, and Chandler examined the apartment. "I bet this place once had beautiful doorknobs," Josh heard him say to nobody. "When a place like this is renovated, why do they put in ugly doorknobs?"

Chandler took tiny pieces of the bread Laura had made, barely enough to pinch a bean or a cube of potato, while Laura, Jo, and Josh tore off handkerchief-sized pieces and seized all the food they could. "Explain to Jo how we're related," Josh said as they ate. "I can't."

"You always make me do that," Laura said. "Our mothers are cousins. Our grandmothers are sisters. Your grandma is my great-aunt Sylvia. My grandma is your great-aunt Fanny."

"Great-aunt Fanny!" said Josh. "I can never remember how I know her."

"You're just pretending."

Chandler said, "Why do people go on and on about families?"

"You ask a lot of questions," Josh said. He meant rude questions. Being with Laura made him giddy. Together they grew younger, drawn back to the suitcase of potential babies that their great-grandparents, whose names were Sonia and Joseph, had dragged from the old country.

Then Jo said, "I think I saw the man today."

"What man?" said Chandler.

"The man who did that to you?" Laura said. Her voice had become softer, slower.

"I'm not sure," Jo said. "I was having tea at Carberry's with Sue. A man and a younger woman were eating lunch with a little girl. He wasn't wearing the same jacket, but I saw his face when he looked at the baby."

"Did you call the cops?" said Chandler. Laura must have told him about it.

"I didn't even tell Sue."

"You definitely should have called the cops," Chandler said.

Jo seemed to be speaking only to Laura. "Monday I thought he'd invented the baby, because how could a real father do that? But every guy has sperm. The thing is, what if he really brings her to the center?"

"Of course he won't." Laura clutched her hair.

"I wish I were sure it was the same man," Jo said. "In a movie, he'd have a birthmark."

"Why a birthmark?" said Chandler. They were all squeezed together with their knees touching. Josh thought he saw Jo hitch her chair away from Chandler.

She said, "When they finished lunch, the woman got up to buy a cookie, which she broke into three parts. So *sane*. I couldn't stand it. I told Sue I didn't feel well and ran out of there and walked about a mile. I couldn't stand it *whether or not* it was the same man. I was late getting back to work, but nobody cared. They expect me to be crazy—the crime victim. Maybe I'll become mute, like the kid in the movie."

"A movie with a birthmark?" Chandler said. Jo didn't answer, so Josh told him about the child who'd witnessed her mother's murder, but before he could describe his dream, Chandler said he thought he remembered that film. "Doesn't the murderer come back and kill the little kid?"

"You like this guy?" Jo said quickly to Laura. "I don't think I do."

Josh saw Laura decide to take this as a joke. Then Jo said, "He never opens his mouth without saying the wrong thing. I couldn't possibly call the cops. They'd think I imagined it. Maybe I did imagine it. Maybe I made the whole thing up." She stood, looked at Josh, then said, "I'm going to bed."

Josh and Laura were left with the dishes. Chandler went for a walk after Jo went off to bed, and Laura explained that he smoked. "Jo must despise me," she said to Josh. "I should have said something."

"I think she's crazy about you," Josh said. "It's me she's mad at."

"I'm hung up about Chandler," said Laura. "Jo doesn't respect that. I don't either."

"Should I tell her to talk to the cops about the guy in Carberry's?" Josh said.

"Of course. It was definitely the same guy," said Laura.

Listening from the next room as she tried to sleep, Jo was surprised that Laura thought herself despised. Jo was glad Laura had come, and didn't blame her for being unable to school her feelings about Chandler. She felt bad for being difficult. She marveled that Laura was sure about the man. Jo had never considered calling the police a second time.

In the morning Jo was the first awake. She put on sweat clothes and went for a run. The crowded little streets looked shabby. It was March, and the chain-link fences were not yet blurred with spring green. Jo ran to the bike path on which she ordinarily walked to work, and then ran along it, searching the face of every passerby for the man with the knife or the woman who bought the cookie. She ran past the day-care center, then stopped running, turned, and walked home past Carberry's. If she'd brought money, she could have bought muffins and scones for the guests. She looked inside at couples with small children, older men with younger women.

As she let herself into the apartment, she heard voices. "Of course not," Josh was saying.

"I didn't *think* so," said Laura.

"Were you talking about me?" said Jo, coming into the living room.

"We were talking about your ghost." Laura was standing, a hairbrush in her hand.

"Did you hear her?" said Jo.

"I asked Josh if you *believed* in the ghost," Laura said. "You know, the way you believe in that chair—and he said no."

"But I do," said Jo, glancing at the chair—her only piece of upholstered furniture, which she'd bought in college from a friend. It was brown, shabby and comfortable. Chandler was sitting in it. "You didn't see her, did you? I just hear her." Then Jo walked past them into the kitchen. She ran the cold water, filled a glass, and stayed to drink it. Then she refilled it and returned to the living room.

Chandler's feet stuck out into the room. Jo would have liked to sit in the chair.

"Do you want to go out for brunch?" Laura said. "We'd have to do it soon—later, we're meeting my old roommate." She brushed her hair forward, then back.

"But you *did* hear the ghost, didn't you?" Jo said. "Otherwise, how did you know about it?"

"We didn't hear it," said Laura. They stood facing each other.

"So you told them?" Jo said to Josh.

He was standing in the doorway. "Chandler wanted to know why we pay so much rent."

"You told him how much *rent* we pay?"

"People are curious about Boston real estate," Josh said.

"It's even more than I pay," Chandler said.

Josh said, "So I told him we pay extra for a ghost. The ghost of a murderer."

"That makes me angry with you," Jo said quietly. She took a sip of water.

"Why?" Josh stepped backward, out of the doorway and into the hall. Then forward again, back into the doorway.

"Because it's making fun of what I think," she said, but that wasn't the only reason.

"Do Chinese people believe in ghosts?" said Chandler.

Josh pressed his hands into the doorjamb, pushing up a little on his toes. "Jo is Korean, not Chinese," he said.

"Korean-American," said Jo tersely. "Born here."

"Ghosts are such a fad," said Chandler. "Everybody's got ghosts. Or they burn stuff to get rid of ghosts. Do you burn stuff?"

"No," said Jo. "There's no getting rid of her. She's just here, as ordinary as that chair."

Chandler stood, walked to the window, turned back. He said, "That's why you won't call the cops. You think they're the same."

"Call the cops about the *ghost*?" said Jo.

"You know, Jo," Josh said, still pressing on the doorjamb, "sometimes the ghost does get a little boring. The man, unfortunately, was real. The ghost isn't real. Okay?"

"About the man," said Chandler.

"The ghost is real," said Jo, and she seemed to feel herself grow taller and thicker, as if each limb stretched, and her feet pressed with additional weight into the floor.

"But Chandler's right," Josh said. "Ghosts are a fad. We only know about them because we already know about them."

Jo said, "If you don't say I might be right about the ghost—might, I'm not saying you have to say I'm definitely right—if you don't say I might be right, I'll overturn this glass of water on your head."

"That's not the issue," said Josh, so Jo crossed the room, and with joy raised her arm (Laura cried, "Don't!") and emptied the glass of water on Josh's head.

He saw her black hair swing as she tipped her head back to watch the water rush down on him. The water was cold. Jo dropped the glass, by mistake, Josh thought, and Laura took over, policing them so they didn't slip in the wet and cut themselves on the broken glass. Chandler stayed where he was, silent. "I'm sorry," said Jo, sounding slightly awestruck. She ignored Laura's instructions, stepped toward Josh, and put her arms around him.

She was trembling—that was why she dropped the glass. She might even have been crying. Then she said, "I need a shower," but before locking herself in the bathroom she handed Josh a towel and said, "Take off your clothes, Joshua." Holding the bathroom door open, she sang:

A Joshua sat on the railroad track
His heart was all aflutter.
Around the bend came Engine Ten,
Uh-oh, Joshua butter.

When Jo closed the bathroom door, Laura decided that she and Chandler ought to leave immediately. "Jo will understand," Laura said. "Give her my love. Tell her thanks. I'll call her next week. I'll send her an e-mail." They were spending the night at the old roommate's place, leaving early the next day. She'd already packed, and Josh stood, wet and getting colder, while she went for their bags, kissed his cheek, and got Chandler out the door.

Josh stripped, leaving his clothes in a heap. He got into bed, pulled up the covers, and gradually began to feel less cold, then warm. By the time Jo turned off the shower, he was a little sleepy. She came in, naked, and got into bed with him. She began to talk slowly. "I let the ghost into my head, and I sing songs that kill the children," she said. "And kill you, too. Did I make the man come? Did I make him take out his knife?"

"No," Josh said. "It's not a real train."

"That was him, in Carberry's."

"I thought so." He pulled her closer and then he felt her tongue exploring the inside of his mouth: the linings of his cheeks, his teeth—one skewed, but the others orderly.

Jo's tongue arched to meet his. "Let's see," he said, pulling back just far enough to speak, postponing the question of calling the police. "What shall we do now?" He fell in love with her that morning, or at least with himself, which made anything possible.

They had love followed by brunch, out in the city where the dead—kind or malevolent—couldn't be heard; where the malevolent living disappeared around corners just in time to be missed; and where everyone else was like them, lining up with sticky thighs for pancakes, Danish, or omelets.

Brooklyn Sestina

Crates of live chickens," said Lillian: an example of what made her wish to die.

"Where?" asked Ruth. Ruth was a student at Brooklyn College and her sister, Lillian, was in high school.

"Blake Avenue. Kosher chickens."

"Recently?"

"I was little."

"What about them specifically?" asked Ruth. It was 1960. Their parents were out and the girls would cook their own supper when they got around to it. Now they lay on their beds in the impinging spring dusk, both on their backs, shoes on the tasteful beige bedspreads. Frightened by her sister's mood, Ruth stared at a plaster excrescence on the ceiling—an old gaslight—as its knobs and petals disappeared in the thickening dimness.

"Their squashed feathers," said Lillian. "The feathers could be broken. What would you call that thing that would break—you know, the spine of the feather?"

"I don't know. Is it cartilage?"

"Between hair and cartilage."

Lying as she was, Ruth could not see Lilly, only the ceiling. She asked, "Did the chickens make you want to die when you saw them years ago, or is it only now when you think about them?" Presumably their being kosher chickens had nothing to do with it. Their family was not kosher and had belonged to the temple for only one year, when Ruth—in high school then—insisted on going to services. Now, she'd recently told her parents, she was an atheist. "Nonsense," her father had said, though he'd been just as dismissive when she'd persuaded him, once, to come to services. Halfway through the prayers he'd whispered, "If God is so powerful, couldn't He make this shorter?"

Now Lillian's voice came out of the dark. "I wanted to die when I saw them."

"So you were six or something, and you were already thinking like this?"

"I was born thinking like this. I found out why when I saw the crates of chickens. I thought *Oh.*"

Ruth had never wished to die, yet sometimes it seemed that she and her sister were a single organism. She understood "I thought *Oh.*" She tried to think when in her life she'd thought *Oh.* She rolled onto her side and could see part of Lillian now, across the room. Ruth's woolen skirt was bunched uncomfortably under her thighs.

Lilly raised a long arm toward the petaled shape on the ceiling. Her hand—just visible to Ruth in the dark—made and unmade a fist as she took exuberant pleasure in the point she was about to make. "Figuring out a good way to die is like using the *q* on a Triple Word Score."

Her sister had gone too far. Ruth stood up and smoothed her clothes. "I'll make supper."

She warmed the meat sauce her mother had left, and boiled a pot of water for spaghetti. She boiled more water and broke off a chunk of frozen green beans to put into it.

"This afternoon I planned how to kill myself," Lillian had begun. If Ruth ought to tell their parents—who would do the wrong thing, whatever that might be—Lilly was being disloyal to her: it would be like saying, "You're not enough for me. Let's invite Mom and Dad into the conversation." Ruth dipped into the spaghetti pot with a fork, trying to snag a strand. She burned her fingers, then scalded her tongue when she sucked spaghetti into her mouth. Then she drained the spaghetti, though some of it was in clumps. She drained the green beans. Some of them still looked a little icy. Ruth was an English major. She could discuss literature, or write a poem, more easily than cook a meal.

"All the old pills in the medicine chest," Lilly had enumerated. "Or just closing my eyes when I cross the street." As Ruth dished up the food, Lillian came to the table dangling and shaking wet hands until they blurred before Ruth's eyes. Lillian's breasts were high and round, and her hair was in supple curls shaped nightly by big pink rollers. She was taller and sexier than her older sister. Her movements were bold, easy—and then abruptly awkward.

They ate. Lillian said, "My spaghetti's full of rocks." Ruth reached across the table and exchanged her sister's plate for her own.

Ruth was taking a poetry workshop. The professor said he rose to write poems each morning at five thirty, and Ruth thought she'd try that. She bought a big alarm clock with a loud tick, which Lillian called the Time Bomb. But when she woke up early, Ruth discovered that the heat in their apartment didn't go on until six thirty. She hurried from their bedroom while Lillian turned over and went back to sleep, then sat on the living-room floor with her back leaning on the radiator, waiting for the heat's gurgle. She wrote no poems or bad poems, but did better with the required weekly exercises, which had to follow certain rules but could be pointless. One week she wrote a silly sonnet early in the morning, the next a villanelle.

The week after Lillian's remarks about suicide, the poetry professor distributed a mimeographed sestina. Ruth had never seen a poem like that before. When she arrived home after class, the apartment was dark. Her parents hadn't yet returned from work, but Lillian ought to be there. Ruth snapped on lights on her way to their room. Lilly was in bed. "Leave me alone," she said.

"Wake up. You have to see this."

"See what?"

"It's a kind of poem." A sestina, Ruth explained, was a medieval Italian form. "Give me six words. Any six words."

"Sleep," said Lilly. "Sister. Dumbbell . . ."

Ruth wrote them down. "Come on, just three more."

"Just. Three. More."

"Okay, fine. Now, the first line of the sestina will end with the word *sleep.* The second line ends with *sister.*" She made for Lillian the chart her professor had drawn on the blackboard, showing how in each subsequent stanza the same six words would end the lines in a strict, varying pattern. In the second stanza, Word Six would be used first, then Word One, then Five, Two, Four, Three.

"Bottom, top, bottom, top," she explained. At the end, a shorter stanza would use all the words.

The next morning, in the chilly dark, Ruth began a sestina using Lilly's six words:

When I lay down and tried to fall asleep,
I heard a lumbering tread. It was my sister,
A person who is surely not a dumbbell,
A person who is decent, true, and just,
A person I have known since she was three,
A person I will love forevermore.

Awakened from my nap, I cried, "No more!
Don't you know when someone is asleep
You don't come waltzing in—one, two, three—
Disturbing and awakening your sister,
When after an awful day she'd managed just
To fall asleep, you noisy rotten dumbbell!"

Then she ran out of ideas. That night, Lilly helped. She liked being a character in the sestina, and caught on to the tricky form more quickly than Ruth. Between them, they wrote something that almost made sense, and went on for six stanzas, plus a short one at the end.

The following Thursday the poetry professor distributed Sir Philip Sidney's *double* sestina. Again Ruth arrived home and woke Lillian. "This guy did it for twelve stanzas!"

"Do you have to write twelve stanzas?" Lilly sat up in bed. She was more cheerful.

"No, we have to write a ballad. But listen to this poem."

"What's it about?"

"Feeling terrible."

"I like that," said Lillian, and reached for the pages. " 'Ye Goat-herd Gods . . .' What the hell does that mean?"

"Gods who herd goats. Listen to this part:

"Me seems I see a filthy cloudy evening,
As soon as sun begins to climb the mountains.
Me seems I feel a noisome scent, the morning
When I do smell the flowers of these valleys.
Me seems I hear, when I do hear sweet music,
The dreadful cries of murdered men in forests."

Ruth turned shy. "I thought that might be what you meant."

"What I meant?"

"You know. Our conversation that day . . ."

"Oh. Wanting to kill myself. Yup. Music sounds like the cries of murdered men in forests. Joan Baez, say."

The sisters began reading Sidney's poem out loud. The last stanzas, in which the poet explained that he was feeling bad because his girlfriend had broken up with him, interested them less than the preceding ones, which expressed an unqualified, unexplained misery. These they chanted in chorus, marching and even dancing. "Shall we both kill ourselves?" Lilly said breathlessly when they finished.

"It would be hard on Mom and Dad," said Ruth. She quickly began reciting again. Sidney's extravagant language was fun; her sister's wasn't. They quit only when they heard footsteps on the stairs.

. . .

A week later, Ruth walked into the kitchen, where her mother was frying hamburgers, to see Lillian fill a glass of water at the sink. "What are you doing?" cried Ruth, rushing forward to open her sister's fist.

"Are you trying to make me burn the house down?" Her mother steadied the frying pan.

"I have a headache," Lillian said. "You made me drop the aspirin." She didn't search for the fallen pills but poured the water into the sink and left the room.

"I worry about her," Ruth said to her mother.

"She's sick?"

"Sort of."

"How often does she have these headaches?" said her mother. "Maybe she should have her eyes checked."

Ruth followed her sister, who had gone into the bathroom. "Was it really aspirin?"

"You think I'm going to take pills in front of my mother— while she's cooking hamburgers?" Lilly glanced into the mirror and patted her curls.

"You make me nervous."

"There's nothing to be nervous about."

"What about all you told me?" Ruth tried to speak in a low voice. The door was open.

"Did you tell them?"

"No. Should I?"

"If you do," said Lilly, "I'll never trust you again."

She shook pills from the aspirin bottle, drank from the plastic cup with which they brushed their teeth, and squeezed through the doorway past Ruth. Lilly was wearing a tight yellow sweater, and the mohair tickled Ruth's face. Ruth replaced the cap on the aspirin bottle and put it into the medicine chest. Then she examined everything in it, and withdrew half a dozen expired medications, brown bottles with faded labels. This house had no privacy. If she tossed them into the garbage, her parents would want an explanation. Lilly would be waiting in their bedroom. Holding the bottles close to her sides in both hands, Ruth walked to the coat closet at the door of the apartment and deposited the bottles in the pockets of her spring coat.

Ruth was not only a college student but a Girl Scout leader, in charge of her own old troop, which met at the synagogue. She wasn't old enough to be a leader, but when nobody else would do it, a mother agreed to sign her name and come to meetings if Ruth ran them. Ruth didn't like that cynical mother, Mrs. Freedman, who sat crocheting in the corner of the temple vestry hall, her every flick of the yarn conveying impatience, while Ruth led discussions of the Girl Scout laws ("A Girl Scout is cheerful") and supervised craft projects she herself had done not many years earlier.

Now, in the vestry hall, the Girl Scouts were learning knots, though Mrs. Freedman said, "What do they need with knots?" Ruth had bought a rope, and cut it into several short lengths. She taught the square knot, the bowline, and the half hitch to her agreeable but slightly bored scouts, while a girl in each patrol followed Ruth's instructions, then passed the rope on. When Ruth herself had become a scout, she'd imagined that the other members of her patrol would read her thoughts—they'd be together so much, so apart from adults—and that together they'd avert interesting dangers through their knowledge of woods and stars, drawing strength from the Girl Scout Promise and Laws. It hadn't happened, but Ruth had retained a little of her wish. Though as a leader she led hikes through parks and organized the cooking of kosher hot dogs on sticks, her girls seemed to have picked up not her own hope but silent Mrs. Freedman's unimpressed shrug. Nonetheless, the ropes went around the patrols, and eventually everybody learned all three knots.

Then the girls played musical chairs. After that, out of ideas, Ruth suggested singing. The scouts wanted to sing not raucous hiking songs or funny songs about the sinking of the *Titanic,* but solos, and they sat patiently while girl after girl sang alone. One girl knew "Hatikva" in Hebrew and another sang "I Could Have Danced All Night" in a tuneless voice with flat Brooklyn *a*'s. "It's supposed to be 'dahnced,'" someone said. During the singing, Ruth noticed that Lillian had come into the vestry hall and was sitting on a folding chair as far as possible from the crocheting Mrs. Freedman, from whose lap narrow yarn tentacles in all colors extended over chairs around her.

Then Jeanie Murdoch, the daughter of the synagogue's caretaker, raised her hand. A skinny child with hair over her eyes, Jeanie owned no uniform, and Ruth had been trying to figure out how to secure her a bigger girl's hand-me-down without embarrassing anybody. Jeanie reminded Ruth of herself. She recited the Promise with her eyes closed. Now Jeanie stood—nobody else had stood—and, in a pure, careful soprano voice, sang, out of season, "O Holy Night." Ruth was startled: startled at Jeanie's intensity, at the beauty of her singing, at the strangeness of her choice. "O Holy Night" is a long song—long, religious, of course not Jewish—and it took Jeanie a while to sing it. Ruth glanced across the room and saw that Mrs. Freedman was rolling up her crocheted peninsulas with extra attention. In the other direction, Lillian leaned forward on her folding chair.

"Fall on your knees!" Jeanie sang, for the third or fourth time. "O night divine! O night when Christ was born!" Some girls—the troop was mostly Jewish—frowned and whispered. Ruth knew Jews who preferred to leave the room during the singing of Christian songs, others who merely kept silent, and still others who sang all but certain words, like *Christ*. Ruth hadn't been in the sanctuary of the synagogue—just above them—since her brief religious period in high school. She had an unruly voice, so she never sang anything very loudly. But if she felt alien singing Christian songs, she was no less uncomfortable with Jewish ones. Where did other Jews even learn those songs? How did they get so cozy about it all, about matzo balls and Yiddish jokes and prayers in Hebrew? When Ruth did sing, she sang every word, *Christ* and all. Now she listened for as long as Jeanie's song lasted.

Ruth and Lillian were swift walkers, and they set out down the dark street, their feet making plenty of noise on the sidewalk. "How come you came?" Ruth said after a while.

"Did you mind?"

"No." But ordinarily Ruth enjoyed her solitary walk, and these days she had something pleasant to think about: the poetry professor was excited about her. He'd hurried into the classroom before the most recent class, exclaiming, "Ruth Hillsberg has had a breakthrough!" The poem he liked had been written late at night—not first thing in the morning—and was about Ruth's mother. In the poem, as often in life, her mother went straight to the kitchen after work, and then, standing at the stove, nudged each shoe off, using the other foot. "My Mother in Her Stocking Feet" the poem was called.

Walking beside Lilly, Ruth thrust her hands into her pockets and was surprised to discover the medicine bottles. If she'd been alone, she could have found someplace to discard them.

"You didn't mind even though I witnessed the heresy?" said Lillian.

"Jeanie singing in the temple?"

"Mrs. Freedman did not like that."

"It didn't do any harm," said Ruth.

"I didn't say it did," Lilly said. "The reason I came is—I wrote a sestina."

"No kidding! A whole sestina?"

"A whole sestina." Lilly took a folded piece of loose-leaf paper from her pocket, stopped under a streetlamp—Ruth thought she looked beautiful and mysterious, standing there—and began reading aloud:

"I put a broken diamond in my mouth.
You told me not to swallow. In exchange,
You offered me a cooling drink of water.
You tried to tie my hands with a thick cord.

I ran away. I wandered over the map.
The diamond cut my tongue with its sharp point.

"You said, 'I think I understand your point.'
You held your hand to catch what was in my mouth.
You followed me when I wandered over the map.
You offered me cool soda in exchange.
You offered me a pretty silver cord.
In a clean cup, a soothing drink of water.

"I didn't take your soda or your water. . . ."

But then Lilly began to cry. She crumpled the page, then tore it into shreds, letting the pieces scatter. She leaned against Ruth's shoulder and sobbed, while Ruth reached up awkwardly to pat her.

Finally they walked again. "It was good," Ruth said.

"I really did write a whole one."

"I believe you. I don't suppose you have another copy."

"No, that was it."

"It seemed sad."

"It was sad. It got worse."

"But wasn't it fun to write it?" Art, she wanted to say—as dopily as that—makes life worth living. But she couldn't say that.

"I can think of things that are more fun," Lillian said.

At home, their parents were quarreling over a map of Brooklyn. Their mother had found an eye doctor for Lillian, and they were figuring out where his office was, their voices becoming querulous, more Yiddish. "What are you talking about, Eastern Parkway? That's nowhere *near* Eastern Parkway."

"Of course it's near Eastern Parkway. Where Sylvia lived when she got married."

This sort of argument had embarrassed Ruth until recently. So trivial, she'd complain to Lilly. Now she discovered an odd comfort. Her parents' sentences felt like lines in a poem; maybe after a while Ruth's thoughts would all come out in poetry. "It's where Aunt Sylvia lived when first she married," she recited. "Where little Richard and small Joan, my cousins / First drew their breath. . . ."

Everyone ignored her. "The map could be wrong," her father was saying. "Isn't there a little street over here?" Her father looked elegant, with precisely drawn wide ears that stuck out from his head, which was serenely bald. He looked as if he'd speak in whispers.

"There's nothing wrong with the map," said their mother.

Lillian had dropped her coat on a chair and gone into the bedroom. She was wearing the yellow sweater again. "Homework?" her mother called after her.

Ruth found it easier to study in the dining room, listening to her parents' conversation. In the bedroom, she and Lilly would talk—Lilly never did homework—while Ruth strained to hear her parents as well. For the first time, Ruth was going to read *The Waste Land* by T. S. Eliot, and she took off her shoes and settled down at the dining room table with the anthology. April was the cruelest month, just as she'd always heard—but quickly the poem lost her. Ruth was distracted not only by her family but by herself, as if a radio announcer behind her whispered with suppressed excitement, "Ruth Hillsberg is reading *The Waste Land*." Soon she'd no longer be someone who had never read *The Waste Land*. These days, though, when she read a poem she wanted to know if it might influence Lillian—either by convincing her of life's goodness or by comforting her with a telling depiction of its woe. If anything, this poem would be in the second category, but Ruth didn't think it would interest Lillian.

"The garbage smells," she said then, however: suddenly and usefully inspired. She got up and put on her shoes. "I'll take it out."

"I don't smell anything," her mother said. Ruth hadn't either, but at last she could throw out the old medicine bottles. She put on her coat, took the overflowing grocery bag from the pail in the kitchen, and then remembered that the wastebasket in their room was also full. "The *bedroom* waste land," she remarked to nobody, setting down the kitchen garbage near the apartment door, as her mother passed behind her, walking toward the kitchen: the phone was ringing.

"Hello?" said her mother's voice just as Ruth opened the door of the room she shared with Lillian. Her sister sat on her bed, a loose-leaf notebook open beside her. The left sleeve of Lilly's yellow sweater had been pulled up to her elbow, and with the point of a compass—she was taking trig this term—tall, curly-haired Lilly dug in an already deep welt on the back of her arm.

"What are you doing?" Ruth said in a harsh whisper. Before she'd spoken, the compass had been dropped, the sleeve pulled down, while Lilly turned the back of her head toward her sister and looked at the notebook. Their mother was calling Ruth to the phone.

To commit suicide, Ruth explained silently to herself as she went—still in her coat, leaving the kitchen garbage near the door, quickly abandoning her plan to take out the bedroom trash—one would cut the *underside* of one's wrists, not the tops. But with lips and tongue she had to force to form the word she said, "Hello?" into the receiver.

The caller was a man Ruth didn't know, the treasurer, he said, of the temple. "I just wanted to tell you," he began—but he sounded harsh. He wanted to tell her that all the members of her Girl Scout troop had to attend Friday night services that week. "Youth Night," he explained. "Required."

"Required?" said Ruth.

"That's right."

"It can't be *required*," Ruth said, a little sleepily. It was hard to pay attention, but what this man wanted didn't seem to make sense. "I won't see them for a week," she said.

"You'd better call them on the phone, then." He had a high, hurried voice.

"And it's up to them," Ruth went on reasonably. "I can't *make* them come. Maybe they won't want to." She'd never heard of Youth Night. Had Mrs. Freedman rushed to the phone? Had one of her Jewish scouts arrived home singing "O Holy Night"?

"It's required," he said. "Your troop is sponsored by the temple. It participates in temple activities."

Ruth remembered something from the leader's handbook about sponsored troops. "Oh," she said. "No. It's not a sponsored troop. That's something else. We just meet there."

"Look, I've been in scouting for years."

"Boy Scouting or Girl Scouting?" said Ruth, aware of the bedroom door being closed firmly.

"Both!" said the treasurer.

"Oh, but they're completely different organizations," Ruth said fluidly. Suddenly she felt able to speak convincingly, at length, to anyone. She held the receiver in her right hand, and with her left, she fingered the bottles in her pocket, running her finger on their metal caps and glass necks and paper labels. "In Girl Scouting," she said, "a troop that meets in a church or a synagogue is not necessarily sponsored. This troop isn't, and it includes girls who aren't Jewish, as well as Jewish girls who don't belong to the temple. The troop will not expound Jewish theory."

"I'm not asking you to expound Jewish theory—"

"I think you are," Ruth said.

"Look, are you Jewish?" the treasurer demanded suddenly.

"I don't think that's relevant," Ruth said. Her mother was standing behind her, listening. Ruth took her hand out of her pocket.

"But are you Jewish?" said the treasurer.

"My family background is Jewish." Past her mother, who looked baffled, was the closed bedroom door.

"Your family background is Jewish," the man persisted, "but *are you Jewish*?"

"No," said Ruth at last. The man laughed or growled and hung up.

"What did he want?" said her mother as Ruth turned from the phone.

"Go talk to Lillian," she said, almost in tears.

"What does Lilly have to do with it?"

"Just *talk* to her."

No great poets were Girl Scout leaders. No Girl Scout leaders were great poets. Ruth picked up the bag of garbage and left the apartment. She was of no use to her sister: she was too happy. She would have to teach herself to be unhappy, but even as she formed that resolve, she knew how far she'd have to go.

What had just happened on the phone stunned but also pleased her. Ruth would be a martyr to religious freedom. Maybe she'd have to defend Jeanie and her song not just to the treasurer, but to the vice president, the president of the temple, and the rabbi.

"But are you Jewish?" they'd say.

What was the answer, and why didn't she know? A person trying to become unhappy, Ruth almost let herself understand, might well begin with that question. She carried the garbage outside and put it in the metal can with its battered cover, stuffing the old medicines deep inside and pressing the misshapen lid down tightly. Then she looked up at the Brooklyn sky—faint stars overlaid with tree limbs. She stood in her open coat with its empty pockets until she was cold, and then climbed the stairs to Lillian, who was alone in their room, her math book open, her sleeves pulled down over her wrists.

Election Day

I met a sweet man named Harold during the Eisenhower years, but Kennedy was president by the time we went to bed. When I finally saw Harold naked, his penis rising toward me even as he stepped out of his checked boxer shorts, I loved the way he looked if only because I'd waited so long to see. I taught fourth grade, and was in my classroom when Kennedy was shot, but that afternoon I made my way through grieving crowds to meet Harold, a high school teacher, in our usual place, an Upper West Side apartment belonging to a friend of his—a bachelor, we said in those days, but the elegant, subtle drawings on the walls were of men. That afternoon, as we made love, then smoked in silence, the men—nude, hardly more than needy clusters of lines—seemed to reach toward one another in hope not of sex but consolation.

"You have talkative bones, Sylvia," Harold said when I walked to the window, still naked, and stared out. "I can see what you're thinking." I hadn't been thinking of the dead president, just then, but of Harold's constant smoking. But I liked—how I liked—his eyes and mind on me. I told nobody about Harold except my sister Bobbie, who's dead. So now (it's 1980; Ronald Reagan has been elected president) to my knowledge nobody alive knows except Harold himself, assuming *he's* alive.

My husband, Lou, is a Democrat, but he didn't respond to Kennedy's death by sitting dully in front of the television set for days. He'd stop where the doorway framed his familiar slope, glance at the set and me while tying or untying his tie, and leave the room, saying "Enough." From the day Roosevelt died until 1963, I hadn't wept over the news either. As the sixties continued, public happenings changed not only my thoughts but how I spent my time. Lou remained as he'd been.

Harold couldn't stop talking about Kennedy's death. He carried around a letter about it from his son, who was somewhere in Africa, in the Peace Corps. In the waning light of a weekday afternoon, Harold read me letters to and from his son, and letters he'd written me but hadn't mailed. I mailed my letters to him, and at times I wrote about wishing I could give him up. I was trying to stop smoking, and I said breaking up with him might save my life. I didn't worry that the affair might end my marriage.

Two years after Kennedy died, my son, Richard, graduated from college and waited with distressing resignation to be drafted. A pianist, he refused to do anything but practice—anything that might get him a draft deferment. "The Peace Corps?" Harold suggested.

I'd already said it to Richard with stupid nonchalance: "Why don't you just join the Peace Corps?"

"*Just?*" Richard had replied, waving an arm. Then, "I couldn't practice in the Peace Corps." The day Richard went to Vietnam, I wrote to Harold, ending the affair.

Richard went, he came home, and he was not physically maimed. Since then his speaking voice has been louder, less nuanced—a piano on which some keys no longer sound. He gave up music and went to work for the city planner's office, becoming an expert in traffic. You'll occasionally see him quoted in the paper. I didn't like the women he brought home—too much hair and makeup, too few opinions. Meanwhile my daughter, Joan, became a psychotherapist, married another, had three kids. She has plenty of opinions. "Don't you know Richard's gay?" Joan said one day, and I said, "Of course I know," then tried to convince myself that I had. I was hurt that he hadn't trusted Lou and me enough to talk about it, or bring home a boyfriend. I didn't tell Lou about the conversation.

I stayed married, but while marching in antiwar demonstrations or otherwise leading my life, I continued to keep an eye out for what signs in a catering establishment might term my "next affair." I am not bad-looking. I have short curls that have been gray since I was thirty-five, a hooked nose—which, I believe, makes me appear interesting—and a narrow, energetic body. When my mother was still cooking she always said I was too skinny.

Now I don't teach fourth grade; I'm the "facilitator"—awful word—at an alternative high school in a former elementary school. We have what is called an emphasis on the arts (I imagine myself explaining "an emphasis on the arts" to a panel composed of Michelangelo, Mozart, and Milton) and we address ourselves to mildly troubled but smart kids. One day early this fall I looked out my office window above the school's back entrance, and saw fifteen blue-jeaned teenagers—all sizes and races—led by a middle-aged black man in sweat clothes. They ran into our small paved yard, and the teacher unrolled two mats. He knelt, then beckoned to a thin Korean boy, who was coaxed to climb on the teacher's back and sit on his shoulders. The boy stood up cautiously, then let go of the teacher's hands, one at a time, and straightened. He hesitated, then let himself fall forward onto the mat. The teacher was a new part-timer whom I hadn't met.

A short black girl, smiling self-consciously, did the first part of the exercise, but didn't fall forward. Others tried. At last they ran inside again, beneath me, as if I were that big old mother on stilts in *The Nutcracker,* whose children rush out of her skirts, do cartwheels, and then return.

I stood up and stretched, wanting to climb on that teacher's shoulders. The scene excited me, but not sexually. I don't screw my staff for numerous reasons. But I felt left out as that teacher's boss, the responsible person into whose voluminous skirts the lithe young people had run.

In the next weeks I came to know the teacher, Robin Stanford. We shook hands at the end of a staff meeting, then walked down the corridor. Robin's an actor, he told me. He also teaches exercise classes, often to old people, so I mentioned my mother's nursing home and he'd worked there, but before her time. He, too, had an old, ailing mother, and we talked—with quick sympathy—about that life, that responsibility.

"But did you visit someone else at that home?" he asked me. "Two, three years ago?"

"No."

"I've seen you before," he said. He has an expressive voice that rises in pitch when he emphasizes a word. "I've *watched* you. I have to remember where I stared at you, Sylvia."

At our self-consciously innovative school, nobody owns a last name and even the kids call me Sylvia, yet it pleased me when Robin said it. This man had noticed me as I'd made my way through the city, through my life.

"You hustle your elbows," he said. Now he sounded saucy. He imitated me, walking ahead down the corridor with a slight crouch, his behind thrust out a tiny bit, his elbows pointed and working. "I have *admired* that walk," he said solemnly, before giving me a nod as we reached my office and I stepped inside, a little unsettled.

I n the old country," my mother said abruptly on Election Day, while Reagan was being chosen, "a woman had a terrible shock, and all her teeth came out." We were in the car. The schools were closed, and after voting for Carter I cooked a pot roast, then drove to the nursing home and brought her home for supper.

"Her hair, you mean, Mama?" I said, although that's hardly likely either.

"Her teeth. In the morning, she goes to rinse her mouth, and they come out in her hand."

"What was the shock?" I'd been concentrating on traffic and thinking about the election.

"I can't remember."

At my house, I took the wheelchair out of the trunk, unfolded and braked it, and bundled my mother into it. Her paralyzed right arm bunched on the arm of the chair. If she could ever have written, she couldn't do so anymore, but she never learned how. She'd cast an absentee ballot that someone had read to her and marked. "I hope she didn't vote me for Reagan," she'd said when I asked her about it, finding her watching television news in a semi-circle of wheelchairs.

"The *shvartzers*? They don't need Reagan no more than you!" called an old man.

"Now I remember," my mother said as I got behind the chair. She has white hair, cut short and straight, and she wore no hat. In the dark, under a streetlight, her bright head looked like a target, the white almost gleaming. I wasn't used to seeing her outdoors.

"What do you remember?"

"The shock," she said. "What made her teeth come out." Her speech isn't quite right since the stroke, and I couldn't hear what she said next. I crouched next to the chair, but before she said anything, a spoke twisting off the wheel caught my stocking and nicked me. I made a sound and had to reassure my mother. In the house, I left her to change my stockings and wash the scratch. When I came back, she said, "Sylvia, I'm sorry, Sylvia," so I knew she was wet, and we managed to deal with that.

"She visits my mother when I am a little girl," she said, when I returned. I remembered the toothless woman. "Her mouth is folded in so you can't see it. She has no lips. It all went inside like a rock went bang on her mouth."

96

"It looked bashed in?"

"I don't like to look. I stand in the doorway. My mother says, 'Come in, Sonia.' She gives me a little sweet tea on a spoon, but I don't want it. I stand next to my mother's knees, but I don't open my mouth. I'm afraid the same thing should happen to me."

I'd been walking back and forth past my mother's chair, assembling what I needed for supper. When she spoke of this far, far event as if it had just happened, I felt so sad that, mumbling as if I needed something, I hurried again to the second floor. I stared out a window at the other Queens houses, then remembered staring at Robin, and wondered if it was true that he'd seen me once, and then I thought of Harold, who seemed as distant as the woman whose teeth had fallen out: part of a past we can't touch again. Standing near my desk, I picked up something I did want downstairs, a program Robin had given me for a play he'd been in. Richard was coming for dinner, and I wanted to show it to him—to brag, I guess, about the interesting sort of person we have at my school.

Richard hates the nursing home and hadn't seen his grandmother for a long time. He and Lou walked in together, after meeting at the subway station. With the same motion they shrugged off their coats.

"Carter," Lou was saying. "What choice did I have?"

"That's what everyone says," said Richard, and as always in recent years, I found myself resisting his voice, resisting a lack of fluidity. I wish I could prove it was different before he went to war—but why should I need to prove it? How could war *not* change the voice of someone for whom sound mattered most? Now, looking at traffic patterns, he studies cacophony.

"You didn't vote for Reagan, did you?" I said. Richard was the kind of long-armed, thick-armed pianist who looked as if he might pick up the piano, and now he spotted his grandmother and pointed his big arm at her.

"Richard, Richard," she was saying, extending her own good arm toward him.

"I didn't vote," said Richard, over his shoulder.

"You didn't *vote?*" I considered driving him through the city to his precinct—an hour, with traffic—but managed not to make the offer. I think Richard voted for Carter last time, but in '72 we had a fight. I was running a McGovern headquarters, but my son, recently discharged from the army, was for Nixon. Now I was saved by my mother. Richard bent to kiss her, and the conversation changed. She demanded to know if his work tired him. "It's not good to live alone," she said. "And who keeps clean?"

"I have a nice cleaning lady."

Lou had turned on the television. The polls would be open in New York for a while and in California for hours to come, but as he flipped channels, commentators already displayed ominously shaded maps of the United States.

"That's ridiculous," Lou said, pausing to glance at a map before snapping the set off. The red states—where Republicans were predicted to win Senate seats—far outnumbered the blue, I saw as I passed behind him.

"Let Mom see," said Richard, who was sitting on the floor next to the wheelchair.

"She'll see plenty."

I dished out pot roast and potatoes, while Richard scrambled to his feet and came to help. As he moves toward middle age, Richard resembles his father. He's taller but has Lou's sloping look: the glistening forehead tipped slightly back, so the grade of the stomach is that of the face, the brown curls. Both men loosen their ties in the evening so the knot rests at the same place on their chests, and they roll up their sleeves in the same careless way, so the cuffs dangle. I'd been angry with Richard for failing to vote, but I wanted to kiss the skin below his elbow that showed when he swung his arm and his cuff flapped.

At dinner, Richard and Lou sat across from my mother and me. My mother can use a fork awkwardly, but I cut her meat. "Here, when *my* teeth come out," she said, "the dentist makes new ones. In Europe, no such thing."

"Or she couldn't afford them," I said.

"Afford what?" said Lou from across the table, his knife pausing in midair.

"Dentures."

"Who's talking about dentures?"

"Mama knew a woman whose teeth fell out all at once," I said. "Could that happen?"

"They *fell* out?" said Richard.

"Into her hand."

My mother put down her fork and raised her good hand to her lips, curving her fingers as if to catch teeth. The gesture seemed girlish, almost playful.

"I didn't know you wore dentures, Bubbi," Richard said.

"In the morning, no teeth, just like that woman."

We were silent. I lost a tooth—the first—a few years ago. At the time I felt old without limit, and until the dentist made a bridge, the gap seemed large enough for three or four teeth. I didn't want to say that. I couldn't say it to my mother, who'd lost so much more—teeth, husband, continence. I couldn't say it to Lou, who wouldn't answer, nor to Richard, who, these days, might answer too simply. I said it anyway. "When I had a tooth taken out, I felt old. And the space was huge."

Richard looked up and spoke. "Like the space when someone dies. The gap in the line."

"Soldiers?" I said, startled.

"Or anyone. It doesn't seem like just one."

He'd surprised me and I didn't do well with it; I was embarrassed and didn't respond. "She can't remember what the shock was," I said. "What made the woman's teeth fall out."

I was looking at my mother, so I missed the look that must have been on Lou's face. "Who died?" he said urgently to Richard.

"What?" said Richard.

"What? What?" said my mother.

"He goes to war. He tells me nothing," said Lou. "Now someone dies. Who died?"

"I didn't really go to war," said Richard. "Plenty died, though."

"You went there. What do you mean, you didn't go to war?"

"What happened to me was nothing."

"Who died?" Lou said. He'd heard a seriousness in Richard's voice that I'd let myself miss.

"Bradley's friend," said Richard at last. "Not in the war. Bradley's friend died."

"Bradley," said my mother then, "is a homosexual."

I didn't know she knew. Bradley, my nephew, is my sister Bobbie's son. "He said so?"

"Everything, Bradley tells me," said my mother. She always pronounces it "Brodley."

It came to me that Bradley might know about Harold, that Bobbie might have told him before she died. "The man who died, Richard, did you love him?" I said abruptly.

And Richard cried at the dinner table. "What, what?" said Lou. "Whatever is going on with you—she knows." He pointed to me as I sat with my mother—like my lawyer—at my side.

So Richard had loved Bradley's lover, and Bradley's lover had died.

"Dad," said Richard, "I'll tell you anything, but not if you're going to treat me like an idiot."

When Lou is upset his sentences get longer and longer around a repeated unpleasant word. "Idiot? Who's calling you an idiot? What do you mean, treat you like an idiot?"

"It's not that you don't approve of my kind of person," said Richard. "I don't think you believe we exist."

"What do you mean, your kind of person? This business of men with men?"

"Men and men."

"You'll get over it."

"In Europe, my father's cousin," said my mother evenly, when nobody spoke for a moment. "They said he liked the boys."

"I'm not getting over it," Richard said then. He was red and his voice was tight.

"What kind of nonsense?"

Richard left the table. Our dining room is connected by an archway to the living room, and with his napkin still tucked into his belt—his father's habit—he walked the periphery of the room, coming close to the walls and furniture, but touching nothing, as if cataloging the objects he was not going to throw at his father—at all of us, maybe. But what he picked up, finally, was the program for Robin's play, which had been performed at a gallery in Soho. "What's this?"

I explained, and Richard quieted, and returned to the table, bringing the program with him. He sat down and took another bite or two. "Didn't we see him?" he said.

"Robin Stanford?"

"Maybe at Shakespeare in the Park? The name is familiar."

A couple of years earlier, we'd met in Central Park, I'd brought a picnic supper, and Richard and I had seen *The Taming of the Shrew*. A happy occasion.

"I don't remember," I said. "I'll ask him." If Robin had acted in something I might have seen, he'd surely have said so. But I liked the thought: Richard and I bundling our tablecloth off the grass and going to stand on line with the other playgoers, while Robin strides past us on his way to work, watching me walk.

"The woman," said my mother. "She lost her teeth when her husband found out she loved another man."

"He knocked them out?" said Lou.

"No, no, they fell. In the morning, they fell."

Clearing the table, while again Richard moved to help me, I made a sympathetic noise with my mouth, but said nothing.

"With a tie on, you ate," said my mother as Richard paused opposite her, gathering plates. "One spot, it will be ruined."

"You're right," said Richard. He took off his tie.

"Let me see that tie," Lou said now, his voice different—lighter. "What did you pay for this tie? This is a cheap tie."

Richard's voice grew loud, but I knew he was grateful. "What are you talking about? This is a beautiful tie I bought at Bloomingdale's!" It was patterned, greens and yellows.

"You don't need to get your ties from Bloomingdale's," Lou said. "I get much better ones at a little place near my office."

"Now who's wearing a cheap tie? Huh?"

His father undid the knot of his own tie, yanked it off, and forced it into Richard's hand. It was a quieter tie, dark red on black. "*Here's* a tie. Give me that tie of yours." Solemnly they rolled down their sleeves, buttoned their collars, and put on each other's tie, facing each other like a couple of mirrors.

"Not bad," Richard said, shaking his head. He and I stacked the dishwasher while Lou turned on the TV again so he and my mother could watch the election returns. Soon it would be time to drive her back to the nursing home. Then Lou brushed his fingers against the loose spoke of the wheelchair. He exclaimed, and Richard went to look. They'd forgotten they'd exchanged ties. They couldn't break the spoke off, so together they decided to twist it out of the way. Lou brought some twine and while Richard held the bent spoke in place, Lou wrapped it. I watched them and so did my mother, looking down at them benevolently, her cropped white head bent. In the background journalists spoke numbers. "How could you not vote against Ronald Reagan?" I said. "Him and his 'moral majority.'"

But Richard, squatting near the wheelchair with his father, didn't hear me, and neither he nor my husband seemed aware of the old woman—now drowsing, I thought—sitting in the chair. I felt her solitude and mine as the men struggled with their conscientious repair together. I stood to get our coats, spoke so she'd awaken, and helped her into hers, raising her so as to ease it underneath her. The knotting of the twine was complete.

"Sylvia, a glass of water?" my mother said, and I brought her one. She's always thirsty after dinner, and as I grow older, so am I. "If I drank that much," I said as she sipped from the glass I held, "I'd be running to the bathroom all night."

My mother said, "Whatever I do, when they come, I'm wet. But they don't mind."

"Did you hear that?" Lou said. "Sylvia, did you hear that? Your boyfriend. It's all over with your boyfriend."

"What are you talking about?" I said. I felt myself redden, and turned to the television set. I don't know what I expected to see.

"McGovern lost his Senate seat, Mom," Richard said. "They just projected that outcome."

"Her boyfriend," Lou said. "He was like her boyfriend."

He was. I loved him, though I never met him, and was sometimes bored by his position papers. I cried when I knew he wouldn't be president. Now I didn't cry. I wheeled my mother to the car, and Richard helped me scoop her sweet bulk into the passenger seat. I went around to the driver's side and he crouched in the open passenger door, his curls lit by the streetlight behind him, extending his good-bye as I got behind the wheel. I looked across my mother at my son. I hadn't asked what the man had died of—the man he'd loved, Bradley's boyfriend. Had Richard stolen him from Bradley, or tried to and failed, or been too ethical to try? I'd been a good mother, close to my children, but I didn't know what my son would do. Richard kissed his grandmother, reached across her to squeeze my shoulder, and closed the door. She'd be asleep in moments. I started the car and drove away, searching the night—with its traffic and ordinary sounds—searching for something to want, something that might possibly happen.

The Bad Jew

I'll eat on a fast day, a bad Jew, exultant,
happy beyond fear of my maker, my God.

FROM "A BAD JEW" BY JOYCE PESEROFF

For one year, at fourteen, I went to synagogue. I liked a ceremony during which the rabbi carried the Torah up and down the aisles, but on the whole I was restless, vocal with objections. My parents had joined the temple at my request, but didn't go there; presently their membership lapsed. To them religion was a simple matter: we were Jewish, we should always say we were Jewish, we should eat traditional Jewish foods along with our ham and shellfish, and that was enough. Years later my mother told me that her immigrant parents dressed up on the High Holy Days and went to the movies, letting the neighbors think they were in shul. I imagine my grandparents serene as they carried out this deception, but as I grew up, still defiantly irreligious, I never became serene about anything.

"The entire content of Jewish services is 'God's good, we're Jewish, God's good, we're Jewish,'" I'd say to one of my more obser-vant cousins. "And I'm not so sure God's good."

But envy complicated my impatience when, invariably, the cousin would reply, "I follow the laws that make sense and ignore the rest. I just want the children to know they're Jewish." When I married, it was not to a Jew. Children of a Jewish mother are Jew-ish, but even after my marriage broke up and I was alone with my son and daughter, taking lovers as wild-eyed as possible while soberly working as an editor, I didn't know how to make my Jew-ish children know what they were.

Eric Teak, a flamboyant man who was not a Jew and not my lover, was the publisher of the Boston environmental magazine *Aqua* when I was its editor. When I worked for him, Eric was in his sixties—ten or fifteen years older than I—with messy gray hair, a belly, and the smooth speaking voice of a younger man. He be-longed to the rich Boston family whose foundation paid *Aqua*'s bills. He wasn't married, not then. While interviewing me for the job, Eric offered coffee. I declined, then wondered as he abruptly left the room and returned, hurrying, to set down a glass of water. Confused, I took a sip.

He shook his head, and into the water stuck a long middle fin-ger, which seemed to swell as I stared. He flicked droplets at me. The gesture was all but obscene but I guess it also resembled bap-tism, because I heard myself say, "I'm Jewish."

"I'm not," he said. Then he said, "Water." The magazine dealt with water pollution, endangered aquatic mammals, depleted fishing grounds, rivers restored to cleanliness. "Can you take wa-ter seriously?"

I said I could, and tried to make sense of him.

Nobody worked at *Aqua* but Eric and me. "How's your sex life, Ruth?" he said, passing through the open space in the middle of the office on my third or fourth day.

"None of your business," I replied pleasantly, trying to decide just how much I minded him. (My sex life was all right. For a few years I'd had a lover who lived in New York.) Another time, Eric asked, "Ruth, do you still menstruate?"

One day, downtown, I stopped to look at posters and photographs mounted on a kiosk: students were protesting foreign sweatshops run by American companies. That night I had a dream. Eric stood near me as I proofread galleys at our metal table. The story was about monthly self-examination of the breasts, and I asked him, "What has this to do with water?"

"How often do you examine your breasts, Ruth?" Eric said in the dream, as he might have in life. He stretched an arm across the table and squeezed my left breast through my sweater. "You have cancer," he said, "but it's a good kind of cancer. I'll just cut it out." He took a Swiss Army knife from his pocket and opened the blade.

"I'd rather have my doctor do it," I said, and awoke. As I opened my eyes I remembered, from the protest wall I'd glanced at the day before, a photograph of a young woman. Its caption quoted her: "My boss touches my breasts."

A few months after I took that job, Eric and I hired a young man named Tibby to type, answer the phone, and help out. My children's age, Tibby had left college to train dolphins in Florida, then returned home to Boston because his grandmother was dying. Though it was late fall, Tibby wore no coat to his interview at our office; a long green woolen scarf was twisted around his neck. While we spoke, as the three of us sat around the metal table in the office's central room, Tibby seemed to play with something, and then he dropped it and had to scramble to retrieve it: a red wooden yo-yo. Unself-consciously, he wound the long cord tightly while Eric stared, and only then put the yo-yo into his pocket.

Tibby looked fragile, like a man on stilts who might fall. He didn't seem impressively efficient, but he was the only applicant we cared to remember after a series of interviews. "How do they capture those dolphins?" Eric demanded of me, as we sat alone, making the decision. "Are they allowed to mate?"

"We need someone *good* here," I said. I admired Tibby's interest in the dolphins and the grandmother.

"Moral or competent?"

"Moral."

"Are we bad?" said Eric. We hired Tibby, who might or might not have been moral but continued to be noticeable, untwisting that green scarf as he arrived, talking, every day. Like my children, Tibby had grown up calling adults by their first names, and sometimes I wished he was slightly in awe of us. He and Eric argued about those dolphins, and the morality of confining any animal. Aging, untrammeled Eric hated zoos and aquariums, however well run, but Tibby believed in the capacity of right-thinking people to do anything right. He did his work, but slowly. His friends visited him at the office, silently watching us or interjecting opinions of their own. Tibby was learning to do tricks with the yo-yo, which looked tiny hanging from his outstretched bony hand, held high above the ground. Occasionally I had to interrupt him with a task as the thing swooped and wobbled. When he wasn't learning tricks, he kept the yo-yo on his lap or on the table, twisting its string on his fingers, or rolling it until it clattered to the floor.

When the three of us were alone one day, Eric paused before entering his office to ask me, "Do Jews believe in original sin?"

"How should I know?" I said. I had an office of my own, but I preferred the light at the metal table, and I was proofreading there.

He said, "You've expressed interest in morality. I'm a Christian, and I believe in original sin. The first thing you ever said to me was 'I'm Jewish'—not that I overhear you praying in Hebrew. Not that a Star of David bounces on your breasts."

"My breasts are my own business," I said. "In what sense are you a Christian? Do you go to church?"

"Yes." He brought his big face close to mine.

"Why haven't they thrown you out for thinking about sex all day long?"

"Sex is part of God's creation," said Eric.

Tibby turned from the copying machine and said, "I'm half Jewish."

"Do Jews believe in original sin?" said Eric, now turning the other way.

"I was raised Episcopalian. My mother's Episcopalian."

It turned out that Tibby's mother went to Eric's church. "Anglo-Catholic," Eric explained to me. "High Church. Bells and smells."

"Do they know life is complicated?" I said. "I never found a synagogue where they knew life is complicated."

"That's the main thing Jews know," said Eric. "How hard did you look?"

"I'm not respectable enough for organized religion," I said.

"What an angry lady," said Eric. "Not enough sex. That guy from New York doesn't show up often enough. Or you're resisting him."

"That's a boring assumption," I said. "I'm angry, so it must be sex. Isn't that a Christian idea? Sex is evil? Jews don't think like that."

"Oh, everyone thinks like that," said Eric, disappearing into his office. Then he stuck his head out and called, "Except me." The door closed again.

"Hey, Ruth," Tibby said, pausing at my desk, his arms laden with light, hot pages from the copier, his eyes bright. "Did your parents think sex is evil?"

"No," I said. "They thought it was foolish. But what are we doing to your young mind, sonny?"

"Don't worry about me," said Tibby, and carried off his pile of copies. When Eric next emerged, Tibby hurried to stand just opposite him, raised an index finger, and in the dazzled tone in which Eric himself proposed story ideas, said, " 'What Do Walruses Think About Sex?' " He paused. " 'What Do Fish Think About Sex?' " Another pause. " 'What Do Algae Think About Sex?' "

"Write 'em up, I'll print 'em," said Eric, and clapped Tibby's thin shoulder.

Tibby took that opportunity to ask for a week off without pay. His grandmother had not died after all, and he wanted to visit his friends in Florida, to see the dolphins. "I'll find out everything you want to know, Eric," he said. "If I write a story about dolphins, will you pay my plane fare?"

"You're always talking about writing stories. How do I know you'll even come back?"

"I'll come back."

The office was quiet without Tibby, and though I had to do my own filing and copying, I could concentrate more easily without his ebullience and his yo-yo. The day he was to return I came to work a little late. Eric was sitting at the metal table, his head down, and he pointed wordlessly at the answering machine, then stood up, making a strange, alarmed noise, and took me in his arms as I stepped toward it. Tibby had drowned in Florida, swimming in calm water off the end of a friend's boat. The message, which I finally made myself listen to, was from his sister.

Eric and I did slipshod work that week. We hugged often, stopped making jokes and talking about sex. I dreamed about Eric and Tibby and me as if we were a family—the three of us in a car, the three of us walking on a windy sidewalk. Tibby's funeral, in Eric's church, was attended by heartbreaking crowds of young people who looked as if they hardly ever got that dressed up or entered such a building. I looked for the ones who'd come to the office. It turned out Tibby's real name was Theobald.

I didn't like the funeral. I felt rage at the priest, who seemed to think that putting on brightly colored vestments and executing stylized movements made a difference, rage at the young people who'd missed seeing Tibby disappear, rage at myself. I could have protested when he asked to go. Our gathering, miles from the scene of Tibby's death, indoors with closed doors, felt misguided, irrelevant, maybe heartless—as if our presence on the shore might have saved him, as if staring out at Eric's complicated ocean could have rescued Tibby.

Eric and I sat close to the front of the church, in a side section. When it was time for Communion, he squeezed my shoulder and stood to join the slow procession toward the altar. Suddenly alone, I watched him advance. He looked dignified because he seemed to let himself look foolish—or, rather, unprotected. He let himself be seen doing what he wanted to do. I was reminded of something and then realized, with a smile I couldn't suppress, that it was of the way a good, serious, middle-aged man—like my New York lover—moves toward you when he's decided to take off his clothes and make love to you: dignified in the acknowledgment of the self.

Eric reached the front of the line and knelt to receive the bread. A moment before he had to, he opened his mouth, and I saw his lips and tongue. I watched him receive comfort from the priest, a man his own age. They were like two businessmen conferring, except for one man's clothing, except for their postures, except for what they did with their bodies, one feeding the other like a parent and a baby, like a bird and a baby.

Without discussion we walked a block or two in the cold. I thought we were venting emotion through aimless roaming, but Eric steered me into a Starbucks. Maybe he always went there after church. "Or we could keep going and find a synagogue," he said as we sat down.

"A synagogue?"

"Tibby was half Jewish. We should pray at a synagogue, too. Would that help?"

"Help Tibby? Or help me?"

"Tibby's dead, and I don't see any Jews but you around. The man at the counter doesn't look Jewish."

"It wouldn't help me," I said. Without further remarks, Eric went to the counter and returned with two cups of coffee and a handful of sugar packets. We both drank the coffee black, without sugar, and I arranged and rearranged the sugar packets as we sat in silence.

"Do you believe in heaven?" Eric asked then.

"No."

"That would make it harder."

"Do *you*? Do you believe in heaven?" I didn't know anybody believed in heaven. The optimism of it stunned me.

"Of course it's impossible to imagine heaven," he said. "I think of clean water, but what does that mean? I would like to believe in heaven."

He spoke so quietly and seriously that I didn't say, "Like to! Well, *like* to!" and indeed he continued, "And maybe I do."

I believed not in heaven, but in the poems I'd read and written in college, in my love for my children—not that I found anything, that long winter, to comfort me for the loss of somebody else's child. I planned to visit his parents but only sent a note, not just out of cowardice. With a magazine to put out and without Tibby's help—we didn't replace him—I worked late most nights.

As an adult, I never went near a synagogue, I didn't do anything identifiably Jewish, but on every holy day I knew just when sundown decreed candlelighting and the end of work. I knew what I would have been doing if I had been observant. The religion I didn't practice was not my cousins' comfortable, up-to-date compromise but some unforgiving orthodoxy, the Jewishness that takes over life: defiantly, I did not follow law after law. I didn't follow them so thoroughly that my son grew up apparently unmindful of religion, but somehow my daughter, Laura, learned how to be slightly Jewish, and unlike me, was serenely comfortable as she cheerfully lit the odd Hanukkah candle, attended services now and then, or sent Jewish New Year and Passover cards to my parents, who received them happily. My mother steadfastly cooked on holidays, my daughter was grateful, and both would ignore me when I'd demand "How could God allow Hitler?" looking left and right over my matzo ball soup. But my mother was getting old, and even the matzo ball soup had been omitted lately. The year Tibby died, Laura phoned me early in March to ask, "Is Grandma making a Seder?"

"When did Grandma ever make a Seder?" Soup wasn't a Seder.

"Once, she did." Once, when Laura was about eight, she had. An uncle had read the prayers and the long Exodus story. Other years, the children and I had sometimes been invited to Seders at the houses of the cousins. We took turns reading aloud, we swallowed bits of matzo spread with this and that.

That March I wasn't doing well. Grief for Tibby had dulled but not lessened. I hadn't known him well enough to mourn properly. I didn't miss him, in truth. He'd been in my life so briefly; he was gone and things were as before. I knew no one else who knew him, except Eric, who didn't speak of him. But I didn't feel better. Sometimes I didn't remember why I felt bad. I rarely saw my lover, but had no inclination to spend more time with him, or break up. Later we lived together, then did break up—but that was all to come.

"Do you think you could put on a Seder?" Laura now wanted to know.

"Good God, no."

"I mean the two of us, but in your apartment." Laura was a junior at Brandeis, outside Boston, living in an apartment with several roommates. Brandeis was founded by Jews, and it closes for a week at Passover. "I don't want to feel abandoned," she said. Some of her friends were traveling home to Seders. "I don't want to go out for pizza that night."

"I'm sorry, honey," I said.

I hung up the phone and looked at the calendar. Passover was in three weeks. I'd heard from no cousins. I couldn't be expected to think about Passover because I was grieving for Tibby, the boy with the yo-yo. Then, of course, I called Laura back—my own child, the child who was safe—and agreed to put on a Seder. The next time we spoke, I asked her, "But who'll conduct it? Who'll be the uncle? Who'll be the Jew?"

"I've been to Seders, and so have some of my friends."

"Doesn't someone have to take charge?" I had already invited my friend Annie, but she wasn't Jewish and didn't believe in anything. So I invited Eric. "You're the Jew," I told him. "The believer."

"I'm the Jew."

"I'll meet the bad man," said Annie on the phone.

"Oh, he's not bad."

The Seder was work. Laura had papers to write and no car, so I bought Haggadahs, the books we had to read. I bought what had

to go on the Seder plate. I bought matzo and lots of parsley. I bought groceries to Laura's specifications: this was also a dinner party. She promised to cook, along with her friends, and when I came home from work the day of the Seder, three girls were in the apartment, and potfuls of food had been prepared: chicken, rice.

Laura followed me into my bedroom and closed the door. One friend had told her that rice wasn't allowed on Passover, while the other had brought a cake—not a Passover cake, just a chocolate cake.

"If you're going to worry about rules, I'm leaving now," I said. I had brought plenty of wine—not Passover wine, just wine—and in my socks I went back to the kitchen and poured a glass for myself. Laura clutched at her light curls, a habit since babyhood, as she tried to organize my inadequate plates and silverware while her friends washed vegetables. "You're right, the food will be fine," she said then, smiling at me.

Eric, in jacket and tie, was the only man at the Seder. Laura had invited her flute teacher, who met Annie on the front porch. They came upstairs together, looking pleased and expectant, which made me feel like a fraud. As we gathered around the table, I imagined Eric looking at this roomful of women. He'd picture us bare-breasted, I decided. The image in my mind—our varied breasts (and Annie had had a mastectomy) above the mismatched plates—was wholesome, not erotic. Laura lit the candles. She knew the prayer in English.

Crowded around the table, we looked in the book and explained to one another what to do. Laura was bossy but happy. She began the reading, and then we all took turns, joining in for the responses in earnest chorus. I kept forgetting to start at the back of the book and proceed forward. Some of the Jewishness felt odd, some surprisingly familiar, and I tried to count up just how many Seders the cousins had lured me to. Eric participated loudly and confidently. We blessed the wine and he drained his first glass, while the rest of us sipped. We ate parsley, we broke matzo. The flute teacher—a black woman with long hair coiled behind her head and elegant pewter jewelry—beamed, saying she'd always hoped to attend a Seder. "This is great," said Annie more than once. She, Eric, and the flute teacher seemed like benevolent parents at a school play.

One of Laura's friends wanted to ask the Four Questions. She knew the beginning in Hebrew. I could see my quick-moving, hair-clutching daughter mind that, and mind the fact that she didn't know a word of Hebrew, which made me briefly regret my life. "Sorry, Jen, it's my house," Laura said then, though it wasn't her house, and she asked the questions in English.

Seders like ours were apparently not unforeseen by whoever thought up the idea. The ceremony itself was in part about not understanding it. "Why is this night different from all other nights?" asked Laura, who might well ask. It turned out there were no more questions, just elaborations of the first question. "On all other nights we eat vegetables and herbs of all kinds, while on this night we must eat bitter herbs." Children were supposed to ask these questions, though at Seders I'd attended, self-satisfied children knew more than anyone else present.

Before long the book described more questioning children, the wise son and the wicked son, the good Jew and the bad. The wicked son asked, "What is the meaning of this Passover service which God commanded you?" It was my turn to read, and I read that the wicked son was to be abandoned to his wickedness. "You," he says, not "us." The others were to tell him that God had led them out of Egypt. Presumably the wicked son had been elsewhere when this happened, leading his interesting secular life.

"I want to defend the wicked son," Eric announced. "The wicked son's failure is a failure of imagination, nothing more."

"What's worse than a failure of imagination?" I asked. I would never change—I would always be the wicked son—but I would not deny my wickedness. We continued with the simple son and the naive son, and then came the story itself: the Israelites in Egypt, Moses, God. The ten plagues.

"The ten plagues are barbarous," I said. "I don't like God."

"A nice God wouldn't last a week in *this* universe," Eric said from across the table. "That's why the wicked son belongs in the family." He was sitting right at the corner, straddling a leg, and the corner poked into his belly. His napkin was stuck into his belt though we weren't going to get our dinner for several more pages. He smiled benevolently as if he were God's consultant in the matter of hardening Pharaoh's heart so as to require the ten plagues.

"But it's His universe," said the flute teacher. "Couldn't He provide any universe He wanted?"

Eric said, "We picked this one, and we go on preferring it."

"I don't prefer it," I said, thinking of Tibby.

"You wouldn't like a namby-pamby universe," Eric said. "Eve tells the snake, 'No thanks'—we get a boring world."

"Hasn't our taste just been spoiled by the world we've got?" said the flutist, but her question was unanswered. Laura and her friends were shouting the ten plagues.

To express our moderate sorrow over the sufferings of the Egyptians, we were to dip a finger in our glasses of wine at the mention of each plague—blood, frogs, lice, boils . . . and shake a drop on our plates. Eric stuck all his fingers in, one after another, and flicked extravagant drops, then licked wine off his fingers. "I *extend* my pleasure over the sufferings of the Egyptians."

"You're a character, aren't you?" said the flute teacher.

The Hebrews fled in a hurry, with unleavened bread, and the Egyptians followed. The Red Sea parted for the Israelites, but drowned the pursuing Egyptians, and we offered thanks for several pages, then finally ate our dinner, with normal conversation. Then, just when I began to think we wouldn't return to the final prayers, Laura proclaimed with good-humored fake surprise, "The *afikomen* is missing!" Half a piece of matzo had been wrapped in a napkin sometime earlier. Laura had hidden it, and the rest of us were supposed to search.

More ritual felt tedious, not just I think to me, but we stood and followed Eric, who joyfully flung open closet doors and even pulled out drawers and peeked ostentatiously into them. On our third trip through the living room, I noticed a book at an unaccustomed angle, and withdrew the blue-and-white-checked napkin, which was folded around the piece of matzo.

"You took so long!" Laura exulted, like a little girl. "May I have the *afikomen*, please?"

"No," I said as the others returned to their places. I was surprised to hear myself. "No, I want something in return." I suppose I'd half-consciously remembered part of another Seder, because the young people assured us that, indeed, the *afikomen* is always redeemed.

"I forgot," said Laura. "I didn't plan a reward. Does anyone have a reward for my mother?"

"You won't give me the reward I want," I blurted out, angry now with the entire evening.

Laura said, "We can't bring Tibby back!" His name hadn't been mentioned, but backs straightened and breath was drawn in; everyone knew the story.

"What made that kid an Egyptian?" I said, in tears. "Why didn't the sea open for him?" I heard myself give a low cry, then lowered the wrapped matzo and crushed it in my folded hands.

The *afikomen* remained unredeemed. After a while I sat down, feeling foolish, and handed the lumpy package to Laura, who distributed bits of matzo around the table. Now we spoke more quickly, thanking God yet again. Then it was time to fill a glass of wine for the prophet Elijah, and to open the house door so as to let him enter.

"The apartment door will do," Laura said. I lived in a second-floor apartment in a two-family house. But I wanted cold air on my face, and a moment alone. I opened the apartment door, then walked down the stairs. Halfway down, I heard a heavy tread and turned to see Eric following me. "We still haven't redeemed the *afikomen*," he said. "I thought what to give you."

"Forget it." The house was old, and tattered rubber mats were nailed to the stairs. Eric tripped and scrambled, recovering himself, and I took his arm. We made our way down the stairs like an elderly couple, the old parents banished from the happy table for bitterness and sorrow. I opened the front door and we stepped onto the little wooden porch. The air was cold and pleasant. Elijah was visiting at the house across the street, too— or else those people just didn't bother to keep their front door closed.

"You can close it now," came a voice from upstairs. "Come back!"

But Eric withdrew something from his jacket pocket: Tibby's red yo-yo.

I gave a cry, then said, "Where did you get it?" I grasped it as if it were holy, an object sacred to my people—as if Eric didn't know what he had—and closed my hand around it.

"He left it in the office. I found it, weeks later, under a pile of papers."

"And you kept it? You carry it around? And you'd give it to me?" I slowly understood that if Eric had it at that moment, he had it all the time.

"Yes."

I kissed him on the lips. Across the street, the house door was still open. I wanted to see someone come and close it. Waiting, in my mind I found a rough map of Greater Boston, with house doors open here and there. Beyond Boston, all through New England, some people opened a door for Elijah. It was an intrinsically good act, I decided, to open a door, now and then, to Elijah. "Everywhere are Jewish people," my grandmother used to say. In New York and New Jersey—my mind moved down the coast, omitting and then restoring Long Island— more open doors. If Elijah or anyone else cared to enter, that was temporarily possible. Eric, who stood behind me, flung an arm over my shoulder and across my body, so his elbow collided with my breast and his hand grasped my arm. "Come on," he said, turning me around. We lingered a moment longer, while the door still stood open to the cold spring air, then climbed the stairs to the noisy dining room, where illicit cake had been served. Eric and I sat down to eat cake and praise God some more—God who could move the ocean aside, but mostly didn't.

Future House

Joan Applebaum, executive director of Future House—a nonprofit organization in New Haven offering mental health services to poor women—had provided coffee and cookies for the meeting of her board, though sugar and caffeine made the members quarrelsome, and Joan, who was taller and fatter than any of them, was trying to lose weight. Maybe they paid attention to her because of her size: their argument paused when she spoke, but then she was interrupted by a man's testy voice, coming from outside the window. "I'm gonna work my way *out* of the hole," the man said mysteriously, "not *in*."

Workers were restoring broken stucco. Now that the landlord was improving the building, he wanted more rent than Joan's organization could pay. The workers had erected scaffolding all over the old gray structure (a grand house originally, later a funeral home) and they climbed from one wooden platform to another, like children in a playground designed to encourage the imagination. They appeared at windows, or were abruptly audible. Joan did not like exceptions to the usual rules about windows and doors, about up and down. Outside the window hung the thick torso of a woman in tight denim shorts, girded by a leather belt full of tools. A hand held a cigarette. Joan could see a belly button, an innie. A hammer she couldn't see tapped on the wall. Nails were being driven through the stucco into the brick under it, to hold wire mesh in place. The workers would then spread new stucco on the wire.

As the meeting continued, Joan could hear clients hurry children on the wide staircases. The mothers sounded mentally healthy but exasperated. The board, which had eaten all the cookies, was also exasperated. Nobody wanted to give up the old-fashioned, breezy corridors and high-ceilinged rooms just as the cracks were filled and the walls straightened. The dilapidated building seemed to soothe, whispering of excess: air, windows. *Plenty,* the old building lied, *there's plenty.*

Pete, the associate director, a small man with strong opinions, had been touring places they could rent. He spread a map on the conference table—an old map, no doubt from his glove compartment. A fold was torn just at a street where two available buildings stood. Pete tried to line the sections up properly, leaning over the table and stretching his arm across, a long white sleeve from which a light brown hand protruded. But the map was confusing, and Pete started in the middle of any topic. "Obviously—" he began, somewhat pugnaciously. One building was expensive; the other might not be available after all.

"Apples, peaches, strawberries, blackberries, blueberries . . ." came another voice from outside.

Joan hurried Pete. It was past two. She had to leave, to drive her mother to the eye doctor. When the board members finally departed, Pete came close to her, blocking her. "One minute?" His wife was sick, he explained, and he needed to take some time off that afternoon to look after his daughter. Joan was annoyed, but consented. She suspected that Pete didn't like working for a woman. Before Pete was done talking, her assistant appeared.

"Joanie." Nobody but the assistant called her Joanie. "Can you just make two calls?" Joan couldn't. She took her coffee cup with its plastic lid into the bathroom, rinsed it, and filled it with water. She was trying to drink more water. When she was absent during the working day, she made up the time: tonight, she'd work on the annual report. But she'd be tired, not thinking well. These interruptions—more and more of them lately—mattered. On her way out, carrying the water and mentally making one of those phone calls, she turned to look at the building she was losing, now obscured by poles and platforms. The woman in shorts stood just under the building's peaked roof, like an oddly clad figurehead on a ship's prow, but backward: a symbol of something lousy. Joan hurried. Her parents lived on the other side of the Q bridge, and there was always traffic.

At eighteen, Joan had told her parents for the first time, but not the last, that they weren't models of self-awareness. Sylvia and Lou sold their cramped two-family Brooklyn house and bought a one-family home in Queens. Joan claimed her mother suddenly wanted a big house so as to pretend that her children—Joan and her brother, Richard—weren't growing up.

"Don't be silly," said Sylvia. Joan went to college, then graduate school in psychology at Yale, where she met her husband. They stayed on in New Haven and had two sons and a daughter. Every so often, Joan proposed that her parents move closer to the grandchildren—Richard lived in New York, childless, with a series of boyfriends—but her mother made caustic remarks about aging people who fled the city. When Sylvia retired, she became a docent at the Whitney Museum, and as Joan's children grew, their grandmother took them to the Hayden Planetarium and on long tramps through Central Park. It seemed that she and Lou had figured out how to be old—elder hostels, chamber music—but eventually, after the grandchildren had grown up in their turn and left home, Sylvia said, "I can't die without living near water," and Joan saw that the big house had at last become exhausting. Sylvia wore a hearing aid and walked with a cane, after breaking her hip. Lou was forgetful. They bought a condo outside New Haven, in Branford, though it was far from a bus line and Lou had stopped driving. "I drive," Sylvia said, pointing out the wedge of sea—Long Island Sound—visible from their deck.

They'd moved two years ago, and were fine for a year and a half. Then Sylvia abruptly lost most of the vision in one eye to optic neuritis. She, too, had to stop driving, and the van service for the elderly was unreliable. "At least I can still read," she told Joan. "Sort of." Sylvia was rereading *War and Peace,* carrying her old paperback to Stop & Shop and reading on the bench outside until the van returned for her. "He picks up every other old lady in Greater New Haven before he gets me," she said. "The frozen foods are melted. And in all that time, how much do I read? Maybe three pages." An ophthalmologist offered to perform cataract surgery on Sylvia's better eye: reading might be easier. A month before the day Joan left the board meeting, she'd driven Sylvia to the hospital before dawn, then waited with growing nervousness for the cataract surgery to be over. Finally the doctor, voluble with exhaustion, found Joan in the waiting room. "It was a disaster," he said. Joan was briefly distracted from her mother's predicament by the doctor's startling candor. He'd been unable to get the lens out—"Her eyes are very old, the lens was tough"— and when he finally did, the whole eye threatened to come with it. He'd pushed it in and sewn it up. "Your friends will tell you cataract surgery is nothing, and usually that's right."

"This wasn't your fault," said Joan. "But she's reading *War and Peace*."

The doctor nodded. "She told me."

In a month or two, he told Joan, he'd try again. Meanwhile, he saw Sylvia often, not specifying just what else he feared might go wrong. On dazzling days, Sylvia asked, "Is it sunny?" When Joan drove behind a huge truck, her mother said timidly, "Is something in front of the car?" To Joan's dismay, the apologetic quaver irked her; but so did Sylvia's other tones, too often. Joan knew that fear and love made her angry—fear and love and the lack of anything to do about her mother's near blindness. They should have held a ritual with howling, she decided, but instead they made their way to the doctor and home again, while Joan's work was neglected and Joan felt angry, and angry with herself for being angry—ever—at someone who couldn't see.

Now her father peered from the condo's wide front window with its minimal vinyl trim, his face a gargoyle beside the evenly pleated beige drapes. Joan parked and walked, waving, toward the door. As she walked, she was suddenly convinced that she looked exactly like him, except that she'd been bigger than he was for years and years, and her hair was dyed blond. She could feel his expression on her mouth and cheeks, and she flexed her lips a few times.

"What's the matter?" he said, answering the bell.

"I'm taking Mom to the doctor. Did you forget?"

"Why should I forget? Of course I didn't forget."

The interior was dim. Something was white: her mother's blouse, under a navy blue jacket, as Sylvia moved forward, leaning on her cane. Joan watched, clutching her car keys and waiting for her eyes to adjust—sampling blindness. Sylvia must have worn that jacket to lead staff meetings in her last job, as facilitator of an alternative high school. No, she'd worn it to meet with the district superintendent. She'd run the school in men's five-pocket jeans that never lost their stiffness. The jacket was too big now, hanging on her spare, canted body, the collar crowding her chin.

"He didn't give me lunch until five minutes ago," Sylvia said. Her hair was white, too: short and straight, fluffed around her face and her large bony nose.

"An hour," said Lou. They'd eaten mostly eggs since Lou had become the cook, and Joan thought she saw egg on her mother's lapel.

"*I* can't cook," Sylvia said.

"I know," said Joan.

Grasping cane and purse, Sylvia walked slowly out as Lou stuffed a five-dollar bill into Joan's hand for the valet parking at the medical building.

"Maybe you could see better in there if you turned on a light," Joan said as they moved toward the car. She tried to walk more slowly.

"Very light."

"I said, it's dark in your house. You should turn on a light."

"We can't change lightbulbs."

Joan opened the car door and her mother inserted herself. Joan made sure Sylvia's legs were inside. She reached across her mother's lap to fasten the seat belt, then closed the door. For a few seconds she was alone with one task: walk around the car. *This is what it is like now,* she always felt at this moment, as if time paused briefly. She got in. "Hi, you," said Sylvia.

"Hi, you," Joan said, and with unexpected pleasure she reached over to pat her mother's knee, took a drink of water, and drove back across the Q bridge.

At the medical building, between them they got Sylvia standing, with the bag on her arm and the cane in her hand, and walked three steps away from the car. The automatic doors opened, and after another three steps, Joan could deposit her mother in an out-of-the-way spot while she gave her car keys to the efficient man who ran the valet parking service: a welcome temporary yielding of responsibility. When she returned, her mother had started up the ramp leading to the elevators, planting her cane emphatically. "Sixth floor," said Sylvia, loudly and clearly, when Joan caught up. A middle-aged couple on the elevator smiled as if white-haired Sylvia was cute.

"She's reading *War and Peace,* and she likes the war parts better," Joan said, but the couple looked baffled, and now it was time to maneuver her mother out of the elevator, past a troublesome tree in a pot, through a door, and into the waiting room. And her mother was no longer reading *War and Peace*.

Joan found herself looking at everything—chairs and windows, the bright day outside—unnaturally aware of her eyesight. "Not many people today," she said loudly. Strangers often took what she said to her mother as a remark aimed at a whole room, as if Joan spoke loudly for their benefit. Now, when they sat down and Joan had steadied the cane, a woman opposite nodded. "Your mother?" she said. "Lucky. Mine passed away."

"I *am* lucky."

Sylvia said, "That's a woman. I can see it's a black person, but I couldn't tell if it was a man or a woman."

"Can you see I'm young and gorgeous?" said the woman, who was gray-haired.

"Sure," said Sylvia, tilting her chin back jauntily, and the woman laughed and shook her head.

When the doctor's assistant called "Mrs. Applebaum," Sylvia reached not for her own purse but Joan's. The pocketbooks were similar—large leather envelopes with flaps and longish straps. Joan took her mother's purse without comment and slung it on her shoulder, then joined the procession to the examining room. The purse was light compared to hers. The walk down the hall took long enough for Joan to consider that if toxic fumes suddenly issued from the heating system and they all passed out, rescuers would think she was Sylvia Applebaum with a Medicare card, not Joan Applebaum with a crammed appointment book and a cell phone.

Sylvia's eyesight had not changed since the last visit. With the eye that had had the surgery, she could see only light and dark. With her other, permanently damaged eye, she could see motion and fingers, but not count two fingers. She could not see an *E* projected on the wall, and could not see an *E* pointing in any direction on a card held by the assistant. "Can you see your daughter?"

"I can see that someone is there," said Sylvia lucidly. "With my bad eye. Which is now my good eye. I can tell it's a white person. If I look carefully out of the corner of my eye, I can tell that this person is sitting."

"Good!" The assistant put drops in Sylvia's eyes. Then she left Joan and Sylvia alone.

Sylvia, waiting sleepily with Joan for the eye doctor, was hot. She'd always liked the way she looked in the jacket she was wearing, but it had to be dry cleaned. She and Lou had no way of getting to the dry cleaners, and she wasn't going to make additional requests of Joan. She decided as she waited that she'd wear the jacket once or twice more and then put it in the garbage. With the jacket, a skirt was appropriate and that was all right: Lou could do laundry and she owned a washable skirt, which she had on. But with a skirt went knee-high nylons and loafers. Sylvia had two pairs of loafers and she wasn't sure Lou could tell the difference. They were similar but not identical, and it was possible she was wearing one of each. One had a decorative band across the top; the other didn't.

All her life, Sylvia had been impressive. She'd been the swiftest child in her family at interpreting America for her immigrant parents, and she was a crackerjack at Hunter College. She'd had a long safe marriage enlivened by a secret affair. Retired after a fine career, she had won a tennis tournament. She didn't want to ask Joan, "Do my shoes match?"

Joan said something that sounded as if she didn't want to sit there any longer. "He'll be in soon," Sylvia said.

"I said I have to move. The office. The landlord is asking so much rent, we can't stay."

"A shame," Sylvia said. "You're not going to get a truck and move yourself, will you?" Joan was a psychologist but she didn't do much psychologizing.

"I don't know," Joan said.

"Hire movers. It's worth it." She could imagine Joan carrying boxes herself.

Now the doctor came in, shook hands with Sylvia—she could see his white coat, which moved, and a blur of dark and glint that was his clothes and glasses—and said, "How are you, Mrs. Applebaum?"

"Oh, everything hurts."

"Do you have pain in your eye—or your head?"

"Most of my life I've had headaches," Sylvia said.

"Nothing new, though?" He moved a contraption in front of her. "Move forward for me," he said. She pressed her face against the cold metal. "Good. Good." Her pressure was good. That was what made the doctor nervous: pressure. Pressure of what on what she didn't know. He spoke rapidly about the prospective surgery, and Sylvia hoped Joan was listening. "It looks good," he said loudly to Sylvia herself. "You're using the drops?"

"My husband gets them confused," Sylvia said.

"Can you do it?" he asked.

"How could I do it?" she said sharply. "I can't see."

The doctor patted her knee. "I'm sorry. I was talking to your daughter. I forget if you live together."

Joan seemed to stand up. "No," Sylvia heard her say. "We don't live together, and I can't go twice a day to supervise the drops." And Joan moved forward and for some reason took Sylvia's purse from her lap, then put it back—an action that seemed to amuse the doctor, who laughed nervously.

Joan sounded apologetic now. "My father's at his limit, but I'll explain it again. I'll make a chart." Then she said, "They shouldn't still be living alone."

"They like their independence," said the doctor. "I don't blame them."

Sylvia didn't like her independence. She had none left. But she couldn't imagine how to make a change in the way they lived. It was all she could do to explain to Lou, over and over again, what went in the recycling bin and where she kept the laundry soap.

"We can fix it, Mrs. Applebaum," the doctor said. "I think. I hope."

"I don't think so," said Sylvia.

When Joan took her own purse back, she opened it, and instantly remembered that she'd failed to put the annual report on a floppy disk so she could work on it at home that night. The discovery made her anxious. When her mother asked plaintively if there was time for her to go to the bathroom, Joan replied sharply, "Of course you can go to the bathroom!" but waited for her impatiently. Maneuvering her mother and the cane downstairs, handing over the five-dollar bill, and getting the two of them into the car, she worried that her mother would mind an additional stop, but when she proposed going to her office, her mother was pleased. "I haven't seen it in years," Sylvia said. Then, "Not that I can *see* it, exactly," she said with a laugh that sounded like the mother Joan had known as a girl.

"You're brave," Joan murmured, suddenly glad—as she would have been years ago—to have the chance to take her mother to the place where she worked.

"I'm what?"

"Brave."

Joan told her mother about the renovations to the building, the masonry workers. "It's too bad you can't see the scaffolding. It's interesting." It was past five, and Future House was closed. One car—Pete's, to Joan's surprise—was in the small lot. Joan parked and once more helped Sylvia. The stucco workers had gone as well, leaving drop cloths and planks piled at the side of the lot. Sylvia hesitated, and Joan touched her mother's elbow to guide her. They'd have to use the steps—there was a ramp, but that entrance would be locked from inside. "Okay, you're almost there," Joan said as they approached the climb. The cane touched the bottom step. "Okay, up. Up again. Two more . . ."

Pete's daughter—a four-year-old with lots of curly hair and a worried, adult look—stood at the top of the steps watching them. "Why are you holding a stick?" she said.

Sylvia looked up. "A child?"

"Yes."

"I can just make him out."

"It's a girl," Joan said. "Her father works with me."

"My grandma don't walk with a stick," the girl said again. Joan remembered her name: Dolores.

"Doesn't. Not every grandma needs one," Sylvia said firmly but pleasantly—sounding like someone who had worked with children.

"Are you Puerto Rican?" Dolores now asked.

"No," said Sylvia. "I'm Jewish. What are you?"

"I'm everything."

"Good for you!" said Sylvia. It was true that Dolores was everything. When Pete had applied for his job, he checked every box on the optional section of the form called "How Do You Describe Yourself?": he was black, white, Hispanic, Asian, and Native American, he said, and was glad to tell you about his half-Chinese Guatemalan grandfather or the black grandmother who had married an Indian.

Joan helped her mother into the building. The door stood open, and as they moved into the hallway, Joan could hear Pete's voice on the phone. "No, sweetie, no," he was saying. "Soon, honey . . ."

"Who's taking care of her?" Sylvia said. "She should come inside."

"I think her father is in that office, right over there," Joan said, speaking loudly for Pete's benefit.

"*Don't* point and say 'that,'" Sylvia said. "Why does everybody point when they're talking to blind people?"

Now Pete's voice said, "Listen, I can't . . . no, it's just—" A minute later he appeared in the hallway. "Dolores!" he called. "I told her to play inside!"

He was having an affair, Joan thought. Pete was having an affair. Not with one of her counselors, surely. Not with a client, she prayed. Pete made her feel sexy, she realized. Maybe he was having an affair with a big woman, like Joan.

"Hi," she said, and introduced Pete to her mother.

Dolores came inside. "Look what I found," she said. "I found a lot of them."

She was holding her hands together to grasp something difficult to hold, and she took her booty not to her father but to Sylvia. "Look what I found," she said. "Look."

"What is it?"

"Look."

"I can't see," said Sylvia, who dropped her handbag on the floor to investigate with her fingers. "Sharp!" she said. "What is it, Joan? Nails?" The stucco workers had left some of the long, sharp nails with which, all day, they'd been hammering wire mesh into place. "She could hurt herself badly," Sylvia continued, while Dolores said with increasing urgency, "Why can't you see?"

Joan thought Pete might feel accused and angry, but he had taken to her mother. "You're right," he said. "I'm stupid. Here, baby, give me those."

"I want her to see!" said Dolores.

"She can't see," her father said.

"Why not? Why can't she see?"

"I need to make a call," Pete said, and hurried into his office.

Then Joan brought a chair from her own office, across the hall, and helped her mother sit down, right where she was, with her cane in her lap. Back in her office, she found a floppy disk, and sat down at the computer. She heard Pete's voice on the phone again, and Sylvia, once more talking to Dolores.

It didn't take long to copy the report onto a disk. Joan turned off her computer and put the disk into her purse. She approached her mother from behind, saying "All done," and her mother stood and took a step, groping for the cane, which had slid to the floor. "Wait, I'll get it," Joan said. But as she came near, Sylvia's white head and her shoulders in the navy blue jacket began to sink. Joan knocked the chair aside and received her mother, who relaxed slowly into her arms. Joan was not exactly frightened, only very, very careful: too careful to think what might be happening. "Pete!" she shouted, lowering herself to her knees with her mother's weight on the front of her body, then moving slowly backward and easing Sylvia to the linoleum floor.

Pete pushed her aside. "I know CPR," he said. "Call 911." Swiftly he felt Sylvia's wrist and Joan ran toward her office, thinking, *Dial 9 for an outside line.* Pete began mouth-to-mouth resuscitation on Joan's mother, and Dolores cried.

It was peculiar, Sylvia thought. Certainly she had been standing, looking around out of habit although she couldn't see her cane—except that sometimes, out of the corner of her good (formerly bad) eye, she saw something, for a second, perfectly. But now she was stretched on her back on the floor, with a mouth—

the vigorous, practiced, muscular mouth of a man—pressing down on hers, while the man's breath made her cough and the tomato sauce flavor of his lunch came unpleasantly into her own mouth. But as sometimes in kissing, it was an unpleasantness Sylvia could put aside—even enjoy—because of what else was taking place. "Love," said Sylvia, and the man took his mouth away from hers and spoke. She could see a swirl of dark and light as the man's clothing and his skin moved back and forth over her, while walls—she could see walls—rose behind him. His voice was loud but unclear, as if the wrong knob on a radio had been turned. And a child was crying. Sylvia felt the man's damp hands on her shoulders. They trembled. She didn't know if she knew him. Something was wrong with her eyes. Now two people—Joan, one of them was Joan—knelt over her. Something moved across Sylvia's arm and neck. It was rubbery and springy, twisted—the cord of a telephone, because Joan had stretched the phone cord so she could kneel next to Sylvia while talking. "Hurry!" she was saying.

"I'm fine," Sylvia said. "Don't be silly. I'm fine."

Change

My aunts claimed that my mother blurted out anything that came into her head, and though now I can't think of any examples, my mother and I believed them, and believed that bright people don't blurt. As a boy, growing up in Brooklyn in the fifties and sixties, I tried—often unsuccessfully— not to ask embarrassing questions, not to brandish opinions. Having few friends, I was alone with several puzzling circumstances that couldn't be discussed freely. I had an uncle, for instance, who was neither the brother nor brother-in-law of my mother or my father. I knew my mother's brother, her four sisters, and all their spouses. I didn't know my father, and for a while I thought Uncle Edwin—a salesman of bakery equipment—was my father's brother, who visited my mother in our small apartment twice a week (Thursday evening, Saturday morning) out of pity because my father had left her. Yet Uncle Edwin's last name was Friend, while ours was Kaplowitz, and Uncle Edwin did not know which high school my father had gone to.

My mother waited until I was asleep on Thursdays before taking Uncle Edwin into her bedroom, but I knew she did—as children always know—and wondered why it was a secret, why he was gone in the morning, and why my father's brother got undressed—I knew that, too—if he wasn't sleeping over. A few years later, when I understood more, I'd pretend to be asleep to please my mother. Later still, too old to be put to bed, I'd give off a stagy yawn not long after supper, go into my room, and close the door. Then I learned that Uncle Edwin left at about ten. My yawn sustained the fiction that I didn't know Bobbie slept with him. She *wasn't* a blurter, she never said they were lovers, much less anything else she knew.

When I was thirteen, our dentist retired. "I'll ask Sylvia for the name of her dentist," my mother said. I had a dental form the school wanted filled out, but I suspected that a dentist patronized by my rigorous aunt Sylvia would consider it all right to hurt. Uncle Edwin, who was bland but kind—initiating only rudimentary conversations with me, but agreeing emphatically when Bobbie praised me—would know a kind dentist. I said nothing to my mother, but on Edwin's next Saturday visit, while they sat in the kitchen talking, I asked for the name of his dentist.

It didn't seem like an embarrassing question, but Uncle Edwin, to my dismay, hesitated, then apologized for hesitating, as if we might think he had a selfish desire to deprive me of dental care. At last he told us: Dr. Dressel. My mother began seeing Aunt Sylvia's dentist, but she made an appointment for me with Dr. Dressel, though his office was halfway across Brooklyn and we had to take two buses.

Dr. Dressel's hygienist cleaned my teeth with conscientious glee, then tried to persuade me to take up flossing, demonstrating by slicing a thin cord adroitly into my gums. I'd never heard of flossing—she was ahead of her time—and when Dr. Dressel came in to look me over, I demanded to know if he flossed his teeth.

"Occasionally," he said sheepishly, but after that he called me "Counselor" or "The D.A." and joked about being cross-examined. Dr. Dressel tried hard not to hurt me, though he had to fill many cavities. His jokes were obvious to begin with and became more so, and nothing he said implied anything left unsaid. Two years later my teeth were just teeth, nothing more, to Dr. Dressel and Dorothy, the hygienist. I didn't know why Uncle Edwin had hesitated to speak of this straightforward, unmysterious man, but decided he must have thought Bobbie wouldn't want him to. Maybe he was afraid my mother would consider it presumptuous for Edwin to advise me when he wasn't my dad.

Uncle Edwin never came late or early, never came on a Friday or a Wednesday. It seemed that if he tried, his car would not only fail to start but he might be transformed into a tree or a constellation, the doom of girls in myths. He'd be trapped within bark and sap and dense greenish wood, or hurled into the zodiac. His presences and absences were unexplained, yet my mother behaved as if the reasons for them were self-evident, so protests were impossible. What can't be examined can't be changed sensibly.

When I was quite young, I gradually noticed that in public life—as in private—what eventually took place was the least remarkable possible event. My older cousin Richard sometimes made me listen to him play the piano while our mothers drank coffee in Aunt Sylvia's kitchen. The music sounded angry to me—alarming, as if it might break the piano. When Richard finally turned from the instrument, sweaty and quiet, he'd flip on the television and watch a news broadcast, shaking his head. Inattentive, still hearing the rushing piano notes in the back of my mind, I would explain to myself that whatever Richard feared was not going to happen. The United States was—or perhaps was not—innocent, trustworthy, and harmless. The Russians were the enemy, but they looked like my uncles. War was always imminent, yet again and again I did not find myself lying facedown in the gutter on my way home from school, my hands futilely clasped over my tender medulla as the bomb fell. I walked uneventfully home.

For people I knew, things sometimes changed, but passively, and usually for the worse. A neighborhood might deteriorate, a person give something up. Scolding one another was my aunts' and uncles' primary mode of discourse, and they all scolded my mother to give up—to give up Edwin and to give up much more. At holiday dinners and during Sunday visits, they told her—and me if I was listening—not to think we could do things. My mother thought she could bake strudel, she thought she could sew a dress that she would then wear, she thought she could take college courses, and in all cases my aunts and uncles were right: it was foolish to be caught—only Bobbie would let herself be caught—trying, or even looking as if she might try. Bobbie could knit—she did knit—but my aunts warned her not to try anything complicated, like a cable. I suppose they told Richard he couldn't play the piano, but he resisted them better than I did, because life at Aunt Sylvia's was not as puzzling as life at our house.

After Bobbie's long-ago famously foolish marriage, nothing she or her child did would alter anything, or not really, or not for long—and indeed, one of the mysteries was about me. I thought repeatedly of nakedly touching not women but men. I tried to revise my fantasies, but they persisted. I didn't fear being homosexual—that would be interesting. Sadly, I knew it was not possible to be that surprising, at least where I lived, at least if you were the boy I was. If someday I found a willing man and a nearby bed, my aunts and uncles would see to it that as I reached to touch him the man would become a woman, a bride in shiny white cloth. "What are you knocking your brains out for?" Uncle Morris would say—my real uncle, unlike Edwin, that mild impostor. "Now, Bradley, wouldn't it have been smarter to pick a girl in the first place?"

Sometimes, waiting to fall asleep, I had a fantasy of travel, which was really a fantasy of action. I'd picture the map of the United States with each state in a different color. Then I'd imagine myself barefoot, with a classic bundle, tied up in a bandanna, on a stick over my shoulder. I'd pause at the edge of the map, then step onto it and take off, striding in my imagination across states that changed from colored shapes to dusty roads lined with lush fields or forests. Soon, though, swirls and dimness obscured forests, mountains, and highways, cause and effect dissolved, and I was nowhere.

As I grew older, my mother took it upon herself to answer a question I hadn't asked: why she and Edwin didn't get married. At last I was allowed to know they were sweethearts. Edwin had an aged mother, Bobbie said, so frail she couldn't withstand the experience of meeting my mother or me, much less having us become her relatives. There was a wordless pause, and I knew that what we were not discussing at *that* particular moment was our being Jewish. Breaking my rule against blurting, I said, "If she's so frail, why hasn't she died by now?" Edwin had been in our lives as long as I could remember.

"It's good that his mother hasn't died!" said Bobbie. She and my father had been divorced since I was two, when she brought me on the train to Reno and we stayed there six weeks, but I wondered if the truth was that Bobbie had refused Edwin, still missing my father and hoping he'd return.

Then—it was November of 1963—I got a toothache. My mother called Dr. Dressel, who could see me that day. I was in pain, and Bobbie would have gone with me, but she had to go to work. She was a bookkeeper in a commercial bakery. That's how she'd met Edwin, when he came through selling supplies. It was a school day, but I neither went to school nor stayed home. I rode the bus—two buses—to the dentist. Despite the pain in my tooth, I took some satisfaction in seeing what the city looked like when I was ordinarily in a classroom. Brooklyn, like Dr. Dressel, was frankly ordinary, with its corner groceries and bars, its brownstones and bus stops, from which old women slowly walked down the long blocks, pulling or pushing shopping carts. When I reached the dentist's office, the pain in my mouth had subsided a little, and I was almost afraid he wouldn't find anything, but he probed and nodded. I was tensing against the drill—the sound hurt, and sometimes the drill hurt, despite painkiller—when I heard something disconcerting on the almost inaudible radio. Dr.

Dressel stopped and squirted water into my mouth. The announcer sounded not like someone on the radio but like a regular person—a regular person who was upset.

"Wait a minute," I said. I held up my hand like a traffic cop and the dentist laughed. He thought that once more I was going to cross-examine him. Then we both listened, and we heard that President Kennedy had been shot.

"It's not true," he said. I thought that, too: it couldn't be true. "Rinse," he said, releasing the lever to fill a paper cup with water.

I filled my mouth slowly and listened some more. "It's true," I said. I unclipped my paper bib. "I have to go." I was about to cry or vomit.

"No, I have to finish." He reached both hands toward me in a nondental way and I thought he was about to take my face in his hands, but they stopped in the air. Then he clipped my bib back into place, and turned to the sink, where he washed his hands for a long time while the shocked voice said "Dallas" and other words. Dr. Dressel stepped out of the room, and then the radio went off. He returned and washed his hands once more in the silence. Waiting, I took another cup of water and drank. When he was done filling my tooth at last and had let me out of the chair, I turned the wrong way and saw Dorothy alone in her hygienist's room, her hands over her face, crying. I left the office, my tooth whole and numbed and unassailable. People were on the streets, and because they were all saying the same thing, I could hear everyone's conversation at once. They were saying that Kennedy had been shot. Then they were saying he had died.

Kennedy died on a Friday, but I remember watching television with my mother and Edwin that night, watching the unending coverage after Kennedy's death. Surely Uncle Edwin did not break his rule and come on a Friday. Either we were still watching the following Thursday, or in my mind I have combined two different evenings of television. In my memory it is the same day, when my tooth is still newly freed from pain, and I am still surprised: surprised that something had surprised me. The upheavals of the sixties were caused by Kennedy's death. Young people who had not voted either for or against him and had little sense of who he was were made capable of change by the discovery, on November 22, 1963, that sudden, important change could occur.

In my home the death of Kennedy was the first happening in a rapid series, a transitional period of new developments—some coming when they did only by chance—at the end of which nothing was recognizable, as if everything had been blue before and was yellow afterward. Now came the first days in which blue was only slightly mixed with yellow, to form a subtly greenish blue, which would turn to green, then to a yellowish green, and finally to a yellow that made me blink and squint, as if Bobbie and I had come out into unshielded, searing sunshine.

The first time Edwin came over after Kennedy's death, whenever it was, I didn't yawn and go into my room after we'd watched a little television. I couldn't stop watching. I was sure Bobbie and Edwin would rather watch than go to bed, even they. Or I considered it unseemly to turn off the TV at such a time and go into the bedroom, and I wanted to save my mother and her boyfriend from impropriety, in case they were tempted. With the shocked, honest sound of the radio announcer in my mind, I could no longer carry off that fake yawn.

So I heard my mother say in a low voice to Edwin, "I have a lump."

He looked away from the television, straight at her. He said, "You mean—" and he touched his chest as if pledging allegiance to the flag. A balding man then in his forties, Edwin had sandy hair and glasses with colorless plastic frames, as if to proclaim that, like Brooklyn and Dr. Dressel, he concealed nothing anywhere. When he touched his chest, looking scared, just as some kind of solemn footage appeared on the television screen, he looked as if he really was pledging allegiance. I was trying to persuade myself that what my mother had said was not alarming, that Edwin didn't look scared, just curious, and I tried for an expression of disinterested curiosity on my own face.

"How do you know?" he said.

"I was taking a shower," said my mother. They spoke in low voices, apparently thinking I might be so absorbed by the television that I wouldn't pay attention.

Now I couldn't keep from looking at my mother's chest. I wanted and didn't want to know which breast had a lump. My mother was a short, slightly plump woman with round, bouncing, distinct breasts—not the undifferentiated bosom of my grandmother or of Aunt Clara, my mother's oldest sister. Bobbie showed off her two breasts, wearing not exactly plunging but rounded, low necklines, so a little cleavage showed. She wore perfume and high heels, even around the house, especially when Edwin was coming, and she didn't quite know how to walk in high heels even though she'd worn them for decades. She had a slightly tripping gait, as if the shoes made her walk faster than she wanted to. Sometimes a heel rubbed noisily, making an ugly sound on the kitchen linoleum. "Sor-REE!" she'd say, sounding not sorry but amused.

Edwin didn't seem to know what to say. After a while he turned off the television. I still couldn't pretend to yawn. "Do you want tea?" my mother asked Edwin.

I didn't drink tea, so the question at last sent me to my bedroom. I could hear Edwin and Bobbie talking in the kitchen, while dishes clattered and water ran. She was washing the dinner dishes, something she usually did not do when Edwin was there. They'd be in the sink the next morning, and she'd finally scrub them clean after supper that night. This time I heard dishwashing for a long time, as if Bobbie washed them over and over, keeping her hands in the suds all evening and her back toward her lover, then shaking the drops off to show Edwin to the door.

My aunts took charge of the lump in my mother's breast. Bobbie was deemed incapable of managing it—or maybe she asked for help. Someone had to accompany her to the doctor, and Aunt Fanny, whom I didn't like, was assigned. Fanny I thought of as my powdered aunt. She was surrounded by a scented cloud, and her kisses made me sneeze. I think I disliked her because she was unhappy, and I knew she was unhappy because more than anyone else she believed nothing could change, at least not in a good way. I thought my mother, too, would have preferred Sylvia, but Sylvia taught school all day. My grandmother—a white-haired, passionate old lady, held somewhat in check by her committee of daughters—was too emotional and ignorant, and so was Aunt Clara. Minnie, the youngest, lived in Chicago.

"Can't Aunt Sylvia take a day off?" I asked.

"Of course not," said my mother. Sylvia—a bossy, skinny lady—intrigued me, not just because she was the mother of Richard the pianist. Sylvia seemed to stretch farther in some direction than the rest of us, exploring the blurry areas of the map whether they confused her or not.

I came home from school on a Monday. I know it was a Monday because it was as far as possible from the day Edwin would come. In my memory it's the Monday after Kennedy was shot, but it surely wasn't. I found women all over the place. Aunt Fanny had come home from the doctor's with my mother, and apparently Aunt Clara and my grandmother had been summoned after all, because there they were. Aunt Sylvia had come over after school to find out what the doctor had said, and now sat up straight on a wooden chair, her big teacher's purse, filled with spelling tests, propped at her feet. Everybody's eyes looked strained as they stared at me. They must have begun to stare when they heard my key in the lock. By the time I opened the door they looked exhausted from staring. Aunt Fanny's powder was splotchy. My mother dropped a navy blue partially knitted sleeve to come to me. Her ball of yarn rolled to the floor as she ran toward me in her heels. She said, "Now, I don't want you to worry, Bradley, it's probably nothing."

"He said it was nothing?"

She hugged me. Aunt Sylvia said, "She has to have a biopsy. Then they can see if it's anything."

"What will they do then?" I said, putting my mother gently to one side and setting my books on the coffee table.

"Oh, they'll keep her overnight in the hospital. You can stay with me," Aunt Fanny said.

"He'll stay with me," said Aunt Sylvia. "If it's malignant," she said then, looking hard at me, "they'll take off the breast." I know now that she said "the" because she couldn't bear to say "her," not because she preferred to be impersonal. It was one of Aunt Sylvia's "he should know" speeches, which I'd heard off and on throughout my childhood. I knew the breast would come off and my mother would die anyway. The aunts had been right all along: Bobbie's foolish hopes and ambitions would come to nothing. That they had been correct made me—for the time being—hate them. I picked up the blue sleeve. One needle had slipped out of its stitches, and I picked that needle up, too, and the ball, and rolled up the yarn that had come loose. I felt unbearably tender toward my mother, while my aunts' presence seemed like the cause of our trouble rather than a response to it. In my confusion I turned away without looking at my mother and without speaking. Not taking my coat off, I picked up my books and went into my room—still clutching the knitting—and remained there, emerging only to go to the bathroom. I never did homework before supper. Now I began solving geometry problems, but I couldn't stop imagining my mother on a table, and a long, narrow knife with a stainless steel handle, something like the knife my mother used to cut roasts. I made myself think of something else. But I had to know *when* my mother would go into the hospital and have her breast cut off. At last I left my room. I went to the kitchen and poured a glass of milk, something else I never did. I was behaving like a boy in a naive children's book, drinking milk and starting homework after school. The voices in the living room were now discussing Uncle Edwin—blaming my mother, as usual, for putting up with him when he didn't marry her. "Now at least I should hope—" said Aunt Fanny.

"Did you call him?" said Sylvia.

"Not yet," said Bobbie.

"Do you want me to call him?" asked Fanny.

"I'll call him later," said my mother. I walked into the living room, carrying my glass of milk like a prop in a play. Instead of asking when the biopsy and possible surgery would take place, I looked angrily at my mother and said in a voice that came out squeaky, "Tell them to go away! Just tell them!"

Nobody said anything. They left soon, and when they were quite gone, my mother said, "I'd had enough of them, too."

"Let's call Edwin," I said.

"We can't."

"Why not?"

She was walking back and forth to the kitchen, carrying coffee cups as if it had been an ordinary visit. "He doesn't like to talk on the phone."

"But this is an emergency."

"It'll keep," she said, her back to me. "Why upset him?"

But I was sure he'd want to know. Or I wanted him to know, or just wanted him. When she was in the bathroom I searched her address book but couldn't find Edwin. If I took the phone book from its drawer she'd catch me. I had no privacy. I generally went to bed before her, and woke up after she did. When I left for school, she'd be drinking coffee and smoking a cigarette, still in her bathrobe. (I knew from times I was home that soon she'd look at the clock and stub out the cigarette decisively. Within a few minutes she'd be showered, dressed, and out the door, leaving the dishes on the table.)

The next morning I stopped at a candy store on the way to

school and looked up Edwin Friend in the phone book. He lived on a street I'd never heard of. Of course he'd be at work. I didn't want to phone, anyway. I didn't know whether he lived with his disagreeable mother. I went to the library after school and eventually found Edwin's street on a map of Brooklyn. It seemed fairly close to Dr. Dressel's office, with a piece of Prospect Park in between. I set out guiltily, worried that this trip would take so long, my mother would be home before me. At fifteen, I wasn't required to let Bobbie know if I'd be late, but she'd expect me today of all days. The night before, I had only managed to say, "You'll be fine."

I waited for one bus, then the other. According to the map, if I stayed on it a few blocks past Dr. Dressel's office, then walked right, I'd come to Prospect Park, and Edwin's street wouldn't be far beyond it. The walk to the park took longer than I had thought, and it began to grow dark. After a while I asked directions from a woman who looked like Aunt Fanny. She looked at me with my schoolbooks, maybe trying to decide whether she had the authority to ask me what I was up to. Then she pointed me toward the park, where the paths were curved, and each path led to another curved path, curving differently, so I quickly lost my sense of direction. There was a lake I had to walk around. I was afraid I'd end up where I began, but I didn't. At last I emerged in the dark—cold, hungry, and tired. The streets I now came to had names I remembered from the map, and I found the right one after asking directions only twice more.

Edwin lived on the first floor of a small apartment house. I found the apartment number on the mailbox. As I neared his door, I heard a television. When I rang the doorbell, it was answered by a girl of about my age. After all that, I'd apparently gone to the wrong place. "I'm looking for Mr. Edwin Friend," I said. The girl was dressed, but wearing large, realistic bunny slippers, which made me think it must be late at night, and she'd been on her way to bed. Still looking at me, she shouted, "Daddy!"

Then, as I began to feel strangely ill, I heard familiar footsteps, and familiar Edwin came into the hallway where I stood, opening his eyes wide behind his glasses. "What's wrong?"

"Never mind," I said. I turned, but another voice spoke, a voice I knew.

"Who's there?" When I turned back, for a moment I couldn't place the woman in slacks who stood beside Edwin. "What is it?" she said.

"My mother's sick," I answered.

"Do you live around here?" she said. "I didn't know you lived around here." Then I knew who she was—Dorothy, Dr. Dressel's hygienist, earnestly trying to figure out why the boy who cross-examined the dentist was standing in her front hall.

"I'd better go," I said.

"But what is it?" said Dorothy.

"I know where he lives," Edwin said, touching Dorothy on the shoulder.

"You know him?" she said. Another girl, older than I, came into the hallway. They were a family. Edwin had a family.

"I'll drive him home," said Edwin. "He's lost. Wait right here. Right here, son. I don't want you to move from this spot." He drew me in and closed the door, and they all disappeared. I heard voices, then a toilet flushing, and Edwin came back carrying his coat. He seemed to have trouble putting it on. Then he opened the door. He said nothing while we walked. We came to a car I recognized as his, and now he leaned against it. "What about your mother?" he said.

Edwin was married, but he listened, then drove me home and came inside as if it were Thursday. Bobbie was in tears, not knowing where I could be, so long after supper. I sat and ate, and they sat and watched me, while Bobbie told Edwin what the doctor had said. After he left, I said, "There's something you have to know."

"I already know," Bobbie said.

"How do you know?"

"It's a thing you guess eventually," she said.

"Does Edwin know you know?"

"Maybe he thinks I'm finding out right this minute," she said.

"Does Aunt Sylvia know?"

"Nobody knows but me," said Bobbie.

"He should leave her and marry you," I said, weeping.

"He has children." She took me in her arms.

Edwin had lived two irreconcilable lives for eleven years, but Kennedy had died and it was possible to change. Edwin left Dorothy soon after my mother's breast was removed, and moved to a little apartment in Queens. I had to switch to the unpleasant dentist Aunt Sylvia and my mother saw. Edwin didn't marry my mother—he did have an aged, difficult, anti-Semitic mother— but he visited Bobbie every day and often stayed overnight. Evenings as I read in my room I'd hear him and Bobbie laughing, sometimes at the TV and sometimes without it.

He talked sadly about his daughters, and after a long time, the two girls began to visit us. I didn't like seeing my mother trying to make it up to them with compliments and cakes. "I'm not a good woman," she said to me more than once, and possibly her sisters would have agreed, but they were impressed with Bobbie for other reasons, astonished that she'd known and kept the secret. "I wouldn't have thought she had it in her," Aunt Sylvia said to me, years later.

My mother lived until I was in my late twenties, but was never well for long again. I became different during those years. I became someone who believed in change and was curious about it, though frightened, someone who could put one hand on the hand of a man who attracted me, another on his shoulder. And I became someone able to tell stories about myself. It was part of who I was at City College. When I wasn't getting arrested for political action—for demanding more change—I told funny stories, or stories that seemed funny at first. The one my friends demanded I repeat and repeat was the story of how innocent young Bradley finally deduced that his mother's bachelor boyfriend was married to the dental hygienist. My voice became raucous as the walk through Prospect Park grew longer and longer, the trees darker and more menacing. In exchange for the foolish, pretty mother I never quite had again—and in exchange for her mute son, poised helplessly at the edge of the map—came shouts of harsh laughter from my friends.

Ms. Insight

A t fifty-six, Ruth Hillsberg still wore her thick gray hair well below her shoulders though it caught in pocketbook straps and perhaps made her look out of control. In hot weather she brushed it back into a ponytail. That way, she believed, she appeared almost civilized. Ruth was a magazine editor, a good one. If a confused and badly written story was an unlaundered, tangled pair of tights, she could find the indispensable smelly toe, then tug and smooth until the piece took its true form, feet down/waist up. And after she straightened the tights, she liked to think, she washed them.

Ruth was not quite slim, but she was used to her body, and could buy clothes that fit without trying them on. She permitted herself to walk out of a concert partway through or to leave a museum after looking at only six paintings, and as she walked into the weather she felt grandly draped, not just in her hair but in the freedom she'd given herself.

Ruth had loved several men and been married once, with two splendid children—a son and a daughter in their twenties—to show for it. For several years she had traveled now and then from Boston, where she'd lived for most of her adult life, to a lover's bed in Brooklyn. Then she heard of a job in New York. Old associates praised her, she was interviewed again and again, she got it. "We could live together," she told her lover, Jeremy, who was five years younger than she was. Jeremy doubted, but she was sure. His Park Slope apartment had only one bedroom but a versatile alcove. "It'll be fine," she said confidently. "And *we'll* be fine."

Once her furniture arrived the apartment was crowded, and sometimes she imagined living alone there. Life was not as companionable as she'd pictured it, and she and Jeremy did not cut up fresh vegetables while sipping Shiraz on autumn evenings. But Ruth had grown up in Brooklyn, and it was good to be back. Her son, David, lived on Staten Island with an indoor cat and numerous cameras. David told people he earned his living selling chocolate chip cookies at the farmers' market in Union Square, but as far as Ruth knew he made money designing Web sites and taking photographs.

Three months after they'd begun living together, Jeremy said one morning, "I've fallen in love with a woman of thirty-four." Ruth put down her coffee cup. He continued, "She's pregnant with my baby. I love you, too, but I want to marry her."

"If you let me keep this apartment," said Ruth, rising abruptly, "you don't have to feel guilty." She said, "Don't tell me her name." She moved away from the table.

"But I feel bad. And I want to tell you her name." Jeremy had black, shiny curls. How she would miss his curls.

"If I learn her name, I'll make you miserable."

She picked up her two handbags—a big black purse and a black tote bag full of manuscripts—and left the apartment, dressed but with unbrushed teeth. All the way down in the elevator, she screamed. Ruth Hillsberg—Ms. Insight—had guessed nothing. On the way to work she bought a toothbrush, toothpaste, and a new hairbrush, in case she hadn't even brushed her hair that morning. Her lover had done wrong, yes, but people do wrong. She was angry because for all his easy regret, he did not know he'd done wrong.

On the other hand, she'd gained the apartment, and in exchange for nothing more than saving her screams for the elevator. It was a sunny place with square moldings outlining each much-painted wall, a style Ruth associated with parents and grandparents, with Milton Avery, Moses Soyer, and Diego Rivera prints. Ruth was all right during the two weeks it took Jeremy to remove his belongings, which he accomplished when she was at work. She would come home to find a promising bare space replacing an uncomfortable chair. She cooked a dinner for David, who'd never liked Jeremy. When nothing remained but her possessions, they looked only slightly meager.

The day after the second key had been left in her mailbox with a poorly written, sentimental letter, Ruth began to feel bad. Her mood persisted—worsened—through winter and spring. She turned fifty-seven, while Jeremy's new wife remained—in Ruth's mind at least—thirty-four. Now summer had come. Ruth didn't believe in air-conditioning, but she had a big fan, and in the evenings she'd sit on her bed in front of it, a pile of manuscripts nearby, a book nearby in the other direction. Often she looked at neither.

One night David phoned to suggest dinner the next evening. "I found another sushi place," he said. It was a happy thing that her child enjoyed her—or maybe it was pathetic that they both lacked other company. "And I want you to meet my new girl-friend," David added.

"Oh," said Ruth.

"Is that bad news?"

"Of course not. But how long? Is it serious?"

"Couple of months."

"You've been dating someone for two months?" Just the day before, she'd insisted to a friend that David had been "self-sufficiently celibate" for a year, after a painful breakup.

"I really like her," said David.

"What's her name?"

"Her name is Binnie Levy."

"What does she do?"

"She's a midwife."

"How did you meet her?"

"She bought a cookie," he said.

"David."

"*What?* Are you going to tell me not to get hurt?"

"I wouldn't say that!" said Ruth. "I got hurt myself."

"You suffer over me."

"I don't!" she said. "But is that a good way to meet people?" She hesitated. "You don't really sell cookies, do you?"

"Sometimes I do. Someone I know works for a baker. Some-times he calls me."

"This woman could be anybody."

"The restaurant doesn't take reservations," said David. "If you don't see me, just get in line."

Next day Ruth arrived at the restaurant before David. She stood watching a tall, narrow young woman with a boy's haircut, who couldn't be Binnie because she was talking exuberantly to an old woman farther up the line. Ruth didn't hear anything until the tall woman turned, saying, "But I should find her." Then, to someone Ruth couldn't see, "Are you Ruth?" Then, "Are *you* Ruth?"

"Binnie?" Ruth said, when the tall woman reached her.

"Ruth! Of course! You look like David," said Binnie. Ruth didn't look anything like David, who took after Charlie, his blond, thin father. She tipped her head back to look up at Binnie, who had protruding brown eyes. Then, to Ruth's discomfort, she imagined dying while gazing at this mobile, pointed face, which had dark hair carefully cut in short spikes around it. No such alarming image had come to her through the tenancy of David's previous girlfriends or her daughter Laura's boyfriends.

"I was sure that woman was you," said Binnie. "Of course she's too old. She was interesting, though."

Hands came down heavily on their shoulders. David had come. "I knew she'd spot you," he said to his mother, holding the two of them apart like someone breaking up a fight. He stood on tiptoe to kiss his girlfriend's lips. Presumably Binnie didn't love David, or she wouldn't have been so offhand, meeting David's mother. Yet David, waving his arms—his light hair rising—was obviously crazy about Binnie. He left a calm space in the air right around her and agitated all the rest of the atmosphere he could reach.

The sushi, eventually, was fresh and tasty. Binnie deftly inserted sushi into her mouth with the tips of her long fingers. Exclaiming about the tuna, David continued to swing his arms in the air, colliding with passing strangers. "Did he tell you I'm a midwife?" Binnie asked. "I guess you used an obstetrician, twenty-seven years ago."

"I had a midwife. She wasn't nice," said Ruth. She'd been wondering how to talk with a midwife without making her own womb the subject, and apparently it couldn't be done. The table was small. Twice, Ruth's legs and Binnie's collided.

"In what way wasn't the midwife nice?" Binnie wanted to know.

Ruth had to admit the midwife was only irritating. "She called David Bunny Rabbit before he was born," she said. "She called his father Daddy Rabbit and me Mommy Rabbit."

Binnie said, "You should have just told her not to, Ruth." Then she said, "Hey, David, should I call babies rabbits? They're sometimes duckies, but not till they're born. Before that, it's 'Hey, Buddy.'"

"I was not in a position to make demands," said Ruth. As brightly as she could, she asked, "What's it *like* to be a midwife?"

"*Nothing,*" said Binnie, putting down her chopsticks and gazing into Ruth's eyes, "prepared me for the cord. They're *people*—these babies you deliver—but they're *connected* to somebody, and connected by this strange object. Umbilical cords have a life of their own. Did you touch David's?"

"I cleaned the stump," said Ruth.

"Doesn't count. When it's still connected, it's alive—thick and alive and so interesting!" She paused. "Then you cut it and—next stop, driver's license. Voting."

"Babyhood first," said Ruth.

"Well, you know what I mean." Binnie picked up her purse from the floor and Ruth was afraid she'd pull a long fat umbilical cord out of it, but it was only a tissue she wanted.

After dinner, they walked toward the subway. "We're talking about living together," said Binnie, pausing before a furniture store. "My furniture is shabby, and David's is disgusting."

"I'm dumping some stuff," David said.

"Living together?" said Ruth.

"My father will take your old stuff," said Binnie. "He'll love it."

"Your father loves disgusting furniture?" Ruth said.

"He runs a homeless shelter. They help guys who find apartments—he's always looking for furniture."

Ruth said, "How long have you known each other? Two months, did you say?"

"It'll be two months next week," said Binnie. "I love this guy. My dad loves him. My dad makes decisions even faster than I do."

"You've already met her father?" said Ruth. "What about her mother?"

"My mother lives in Denver. He hasn't met my mother."

"Don't worry," David said, turning from the spare, brilliantly lit sofas in the window and patting Ruth's shoulder. "You're the first mother." They walked her to her subway stop, then said good-bye. Ruth descended with a wave. Everything she'd said had been wrong, and nothing she ought to have said had been spoken. She'd made some terrible mistake when she brought up David, or he'd never have cared for this woman. Subway platforms are not invariably images of loneliness, but this one was.

I'm moving in with Binnie on Saturday," said David, not long after, on the phone.

"I hope you're not getting into the same shit I did," Ruth said.

"Yeah," he said, "you're not a great romance role model."

"Shall I help you move?"

"Oh, no. Binnie will help, and her father is bringing a van from the shelter."

"I want to. Get plenty of boxes." Then, "Come to dinner by yourself," she said, "before you move."

"You don't like her," said David.

"I do."

"You don't, but I do," he said.

"Will you come to dinner?" But David had no time.

The morning of the move was hot, so Ruth put her hair into a ponytail. She was in a bad mood, and though the harbor was healthy with purpose, and the ride on the ferry breezy, she stayed that way. She took a bus to the apartment David was leaving, on the second floor of an old frame house. He'd done no packing. Shadow, a gray cat with a thick tail, inserted himself between Ruth's legs, purring imperiously. "Is Binnie coming?" she asked.

"She has to work. We'll meet her at her place."

"So it's just you and me?" said Ruth.

"And Bob. Binnie's father. He's bringing the van."

"Bob," said Ruth.

"You hate the name Bob?"

As Ruth put David's books into boxes, she asked herself what she wanted. She didn't think David and Binnie would stay together—despite the startling image of herself, dying and staring into those brown eyes—but it would do her son no permanent harm to live with her. She wasn't hurt that he'd kept Binnie a secret for two months. But she wanted to have guessed—to have looked at him, talked to him, and known.

There were many books. Nobody but Ruth ever got enough boxes. She threw away photography magazines without asking, then pulled them from the trash and asked. "No, I need that," said David. She stared at his prints. He'd been photographing Binnie, she saw, and Shadow, and maybe his Staten Island neighbors— people who looked Irish and Italian, leaning over barbecue grills or getting out of cars.

David left in his car to find more boxes. Ruth began working in the kitchen. As she emptied a cabinet, Shadow leaped to the counter, grunting, and shoved her arm. David had a thirty-year-old chipped orange enamel colander with feet that Ruth remembered giving him, after using it herself for years; it had been a wedding present. The kitchen was hot. Ruth found ice water, then began emptying the refrigerator. She filled two garbage bags, then decided to carry the trash out. Holding the first bag, she opened the apartment door, using her foot to guide Shadow away. She pulled the door almost shut behind her, careful not to lock herself out.

She carried the bag downstairs, set it next to a couple of garbage cans, and returned, leaving the house door standing open. But as soon as she opened the apartment door, a gray blur rushed past her downstairs. Ruth felt Shadow's tail brush her leg, grabbed at it, and watched the cat disappear through the doorway.

Fifteen minutes later, she met David as he got out of his car. "Something terrible. Shadow got out."

"Is he—dead?" he said instantly, his voice breaking, gesturing toward the street.

"Oh, honey, *no*—but I can't find him." She told him what had happened.

"But how could you leave the door open?" he said.

Ruth couldn't speak.

"Shit," he said. "Shit, shit, shit."

He was sweaty; the air conditioning in his car was broken. He searched the same shrubbery Ruth had been searching. "There's no point in looking," he said. They went upstairs, where David took off his shirt, shoes, and socks, and began taping boxes together with angry energy. He was thin, younger looking without a shirt. Every little while he'd go downstairs again. Through the window Ruth watched him search. The second time, he returned limping. "I got a splinter," he said. He sat down and picked at his heel.

Ruth couldn't bring herself to offer to help, but David said, "Would you look at it?" He lay down and lifted his foot. The splinter was deep. "Just get a knife and dig it out," he said. Then he remembered that he owned tweezers, but the splinter was too deep to reach.

"Do you have a needle?" she said. Ordinarily she'd be all but weepy with gratitude, allowed to remove her grown-up son's splinter, but now she kept reliving the moment when she snatched at the cat's tail. She was unforgivable. For a year or more, she considered, she'd had no judgment and no sense, and everyone had known it and fled, now even the cat.

David had a needle. Ruth stuck the point into the flame of the gas stove, because her mother had done that. She sat on the edge of the sofa and grasped his heel. She pressed the sharp point of the needle into his skin and began to dig, though she was afraid of hurting him. "Hey!" said David.

"I'm sorry. I'm sorry."

"Just do it." She almost had the point of the needle under the end of the splinter. Someone was on the stairs. "Anybody home?" said the person who had to be Bob.

Not looking up, Ruth pressed an elbow onto David's leg, to keep him where she had him.

"Hi," said David, and Ruth turned her head to see a gray-haired, shaggy man, who started to close the door.

"Leave it open, Bob, would you?" said David as Ruth brought the tip of the splinter out of his skin.

"Hi, Bob," she said. "Would you hand me those tweezers?" She gestured with her chin.

Bob handed her the tweezers and bent over to watch. "This is my mom, Ruth," said David. "Unfortunately she let my cat out."

The splinter—enormous, for a splinter—came out. They passed it around, Ruth to David, David to Bob, Bob to Ruth. Bob's hand was callused and lined. "Should I go look for the cat?" he said.

"No point," said David.

Bob looked as if he'd take charge, but he nodded, then waited for mother or son to tell him what to do. If they couldn't find the cat—if she and David were going to have this between them forever—Ruth at least needed to make the coupling of David and Binnie—misbegotten or not—happen. Maybe it would symbolically complete her own uncoupling at last. She had packed no boxes when she and her lover separated, strained her back on no furniture. Ruth needed to carry furniture so as to arrive at the next segment of her life, and possibly she needed to drop it on the toes of these two men, to complete her own undoing.

Bob's shelter was in Brooklyn, and some furniture was going

there. It would come out of the van first, Ruth pointed out briskly, so it should go in last. She told David it was time to make some decisions, and at last she and Bob picked up an upholstered blue chair and maneuvered it downstairs. By the time they shoved the blue chair into the back corner of the van, they'd had two polite disagreements on the best way to move a wide chair through a narrow doorway. They climbed the stairs again and took the desk. Ruth rather liked carrying furniture with this man, whose arms and body she appreciated.

The three of them filled the van, then David's car. David went for sandwiches and they ate. He returned, a long time later, looking disappointed. Obviously he'd been driving up and down the neighborhood streets. Now it seemed to make sense for Ruth and Bob to go to the shelter, leaving David behind. "You'll see where I work," Bob said, as if they were friends. The van was air conditioned. It smelled of cigarettes, but Bob didn't light up. Ruth sank into the stained seat, with nothing to do, at last—nothing she *could* do—but finger the heavy seat belt buckle in her lap.

"This is good of you," she said.

"I like going to Binnie's place. Fix something, carry something."

"I wish I could do more for David," she said. "Or do less. I wish I could be useful."

"Aren't you?"

"I thought I'd be so helpful today, but all I did was let the cat run away."

"It'll come back," he said. He was either a wise man, or a pest. He continued, "You've got to know something they need. What do you know?"

He sounded irritatingly pleased with himself. "I know editing," she said.

"Well, that will come up. Plumbing is good."

"You know plumbing?"

"The shelter's in an old building."

They crossed the Verrazano Bridge—distanced by the air conditioning, the bright day looked perfect—and soon left the highway. Ruth the Brooklynite was quickly lost as they drove down shabby streets, making many turns while her son's furniture shifted behind her. At last they drew into the driveway of a former elementary school. Men stood around the steps and the door. "We let them in at five," said Bob.

As soon as they opened their doors to the afternoon heat, an old man came toward them. "Look at this, Bob," he said. "Look at this." He unfolded a map. Bob slowly got out of the van. It was hot in the driveway, but before they could move, this old man and his map must be scrutinized. It was a bus map, Ruth saw, and Bob studied it as if it mattered. "This is a crime," said the man.

"What's a crime, Hank?"

"Either the map is wrong or the driver is wrong. In this heat. At my age. I'm fifty-seven, Bob." Ruth stared at him. They were the same age.

The bus had turned at the wrong corner, lengthening Hank's walk. "You gotta do something, Bob. Either they changed the bus route or the driver is loco."

Bob nodded vaguely. "Thanks, Hank," he said, giving back the map. The man started to speak again, but Bob's cell phone rang, and he pointed, ducked his head, and moved to a corner of the yard to talk. Ruth waited, tired and hot. He returned. "Looks like we're stuck," he said to Ruth. "Somebody's having a baby."

"That was Binnie?"

"She can't get away," he said.

"You don't have a key to her place?" said Ruth.

"She won't be long," he said.

"Can I at least have a glass of water?" Ruth said.

"Oh, my woman," Bob said, "what have I done? I've left you to roast here."

"I'm not your woman," said Ruth.

"Every woman is my woman." He laid his hand lightly on her shoulder and steered her into the building, through corridors and down stairs to a cool, dim kitchen. Glasses stood in a dish drainer on the sink. Ruth ran the cold water, filled one, drank it, filled another, leaned over the sink, and poured it over her head. The water felt good on her scalp. She washed her face and arms with a scrap of soap. A roll of paper towels was next to the sink. She dried herself—while Bob stared—then searched in her purse for her hairbrush, pulled off the ponytail holder, and brushed her wet hair. She didn't care about him, so he could watch her wash her face. She did like his arms and hands. He was smiling slightly.

"What?" she said.

"Do you always do that?"

"Pour water on my head?" He nodded. "Only when I'm hot."

"Do it again," he said, and she stared back at him, at those same round brown protruding eyes his daughter had. Then he reached out with one forefinger and lightly tapped the back of her left palm.

"Now what?" she said, but something quivered within her. Her nipples, her crotch registered his touch.

"Let me put you in my office," Bob said. "The guys and I will carry in the furniture." More stairs, more corridors, and he unlocked a musty room, opened a window, turned on a fan, and left her. Ruth sat at his desk, next to the window, on his battered metal swivel chair, mildly swiveling and doing nothing else, for a long time.

Then she examined the desk. On it was a computer, turned off, and a partially written memo in handwriting on a yellow pad. "Pursuant to policies adopted at the last coalition meeting July 10, all staff should be advised that privacy policy implementation forms must be completed by special needs individuals whenever possible and completed by staff and signed by special needs individuals if this is not possible, which is a nuisance but worth it for reasons discussed."

It was an appalling sentence. What a relief to be able to edit something. As Ruth worked, she could hear Bob and the men talking and joking while they carried furniture. She read the memo again, trying to figure out what it meant. After several trials she wrote, "As you know, you now must ask clients to fill out the annoying but important forms explaining how we protect their privacy. At the meeting of the coalition on July 10, the members decided that when clients can't fill out the forms, you should fill them out and ask the clients to sign them."

As she continued to fuss with the sentences, the rise and fall of jocular voices became louder and tenser. She swiveled her chair—this must be how Bob ran the place, turning his chair and looking out the window—and watched. A thin black man, walking with a cane, was talking to Bob. "And I tell you, you are definitely to blame for this!" he said in a low, sonorous voice. The voice carried, and everybody turned to watch.

"So you're still mad at me, Carmichael?" Bob said.

"I shall be mad forever," said the man.

"You know, I have no idea what I did."

"You did evil."

"I do evil all the time. You need to tell me which evil, exactly."

"You know which evil." The man now turned so his back was toward the building, and after that she couldn't hear anything. Curious, she'd paid attention—first to this place, then to Bob, then to his memo, then to the man with the cane. Now as she stopped listening, something tightened in her chest, and she remembered Shadow; again she felt the brush of his tail. At worst, she'd spoiled her life in that neglectful moment. If the cat was gone, if David couldn't forgive her . . . There was a phone on the desk. She thought of calling her daughter, Laura, busy at work in Washington, D.C., just to say, "*You* don't hate me, do you?"

But she called David.

"He came back," he said as soon as he heard her voice. "Shadow walked in the door twenty minutes ago."

"Oh, David. Oh, David." She started to cry.

"I know." He sounded teary as well. "He's smarter than any of us."

Ruth heard Bob coming down the corridor. "Did you hear from Binnie?" she said to David. "She's going to be late."

"I know. It gives me more time. I'm cleaning."

"You all right?" Bob said, opening the door.

"Did you do evil?" she said. Then to David, "Okay, sweetie."

"Okay." She hung up, and turned to face Bob. "The cat came home."

"I thought it would."

"Did you do evil?" she asked again.

"Probably."

"Is that a habit of yours?"

Bob paused, more serious than she'd expected. "I wouldn't go so far as to say a habit. What's that?" He stood behind her, one hand on her shoulder, looking at the pad. "You can't say 'client,' " he said.

"Why not?"

"Stigmatizing. Also, 'special needs individuals' means something."

"But it's not English."

He sighed. "We'll talk about it."

"But it's okay on the whole?" she said.

"Oh, it's much better. Let's get coffee. There's a place not too far." Ruth pulled her hair into a ponytail again, and followed him down the stairs and out of the building. A breeze had started up. She said, "Tell me about this evil you do." It would take time. They had plenty of time to be friends, she reflected, because they probably shouldn't be lovers until after the kids broke up—and maybe got over breaking up. And for all she knew he had someone already. More time. Could she take a lover who was such a bad writer? He was worse than her last lover.

He looked at her. "Do you mind if I smoke in the van?" he said.

She did mind. "Do you mind if I mind?"

"Yes, but all right. I'll do it here." He pulled a pack of cigarettes from his back pocket, turned out of the breeze to strike a match, and inserted a cigarette between his lips. He had a dark mustache, but it was cut short, so she could see that his mouth was wide, his lips pleasantly full. It would take time, as well, to get him to quit smoking. Bob stamped out his cigarette in the littered driveway. "I drink, too," he said.

"So do I. A lot?"

"You'll decide." They climbed into the van and she fastened her seat belt. So did he. He twisted his body to look behind him as he backed out of the driveway. They drove to an old luncheonette. She had iced coffee, he had hot. Tired, they spoke little. He called Binnie, who was on her way home, and they returned to the van. He knew half a dozen shortcuts on the way to his daughter's place, and knew where to park. Leaving the furniture for now, they walked with long matched strides in the cool air, arms and legs light, legs fully extended, as if they imitated horses. Their left legs stepped forward in the same plane, then their right, as if horses paced as one—gaily painted carousel horses, or even live horses.

Boy in Winter

My first lover, James, died of AIDS many years ago, before *The New York Times* had noticed the epidemic. Gay men were dying, some had Kaposi's syndrome—that was all anyone could say so far. My cousin Richard worked for the city, and I knew from him that people in the health department were beginning to be alarmed. Richard was in love with James, we all knew that, but he was *Richard,* who took my hand to cross me when I was a little boy, who once—he was eleven, I was six—flung himself upon me, so we both fell to a subway floor, to keep me from running off a train in confused panic at the wrong stop.

Richard came often to visit James and me. He'd grasp one of us by the arm. "Brad," he'd say. "James, Brad, James . . ." James and I weren't a happy, stable couple except in Richard's mind. He was mourning *us,* reminding himself we *were* a couple, firming his determination to keep his nonsecret a secret. I don't think he acknowledged to himself that he was gay until he fell in love with James. For me, caring for James was something like caring for my mother, who had died not long before of cancer. I gave the intimate help that sick people require, and in both instances, as I did so I often caught myself murmuring the same unplanned words, not to my mother or to James but to myself: "Soon over, no matter, soon over, no matter." I couldn't have said what I thought would soon be over, or what didn't matter.

Two years after James died, I met Warren Beckwirth, who designed the cover of my first book, about changes in the Brooklyn neighborhood where I grew up. Change became my subject, and later I wrote two more books about how communities had become different, but what drew me to Warren might have been a look of permanence. The day we met, as he rummaged in the confusion of his office, I stood behind him and noticed his big feet in heavy shoes, his thick legs, held slightly apart, as if Warren expected gusts of wind to pass through my publisher's art department, wind that would not topple him.

The year Warren and I began living together, he brought me home for Christmas. The trip was a novelty for me, a New York Jew. His parents, Beverly and Warren Sr., lived in Wanda, Wisconsin, where they shrewdly ran a small business, making canvas bags of ingenious design that sold mostly through ads in the back pages of *Yankee* and *The New Yorker*. They were parents so clear-eyed they'd accepted their son's homosexuality without protest, only attentive head shakings. Once something made sense to the Beckwirths, they couldn't oppose it. I was enthralled by them and by Wanda, where people smiled at me in what seemed like a sad and quiet way, and within days the Beckwirths and I were persuading Warren to move to Wanda with me and run the business, so his parents could retire to a one-story condo in North Carolina. Beverly's sweet logic made me weep, and Warren Sr. called me "son." My own father had left my mother and me when I was a baby. Eventually Warren agreed that he might be happier running Bags of Wisconsin than working in the art department of a publisher that, rumor had it, was about to be sold to a larger one, which would have its own art department and might well dump Warren. So we moved.

I was writing about change in Healdsburg, California, once a dusty town of migrant farmworkers, now a chic setting for wineries and tourists. I flew there occasionally, and wrote up my notes in the old green frame house we bought from Warren's parents. Warren had entered my life encumbered with an antique oak desk and swivel chair, acquired in an adventure involving a former lover and a country auction. The desk had scarcely fit in our New York apartment and Warren never wrote at it, but I loved it, and sometimes spread my note cards on it, taking pleasure in its solidity and proportions. Now the desk was a grand presence in our Wisconsin dining room, glowing in afternoon sunlight. We bought a German shepherd puppy named Gloria, and every morning we'd run a few miles with Glory. When we reached the turnoff to Bags of Wisconsin's small cinder-block headquarters, in which Warren had installed a shower, he'd leave Glory and me and run down a hill to greet his employees, who were led by two geniuses, both named Betty. Home in our airy house, with squeaky varnished floorboards and maple trees outside, I'd pace and mumble my sentences into existence while Glory slept. At my computer was an office chair with lumbar support, but I spent

hours in Warren's oak armchair, my feet on a windowsill, shuf-
fling note cards. When my book was published I began one about
Wanda, which used to be a market town and was now vaguely
suburban, vaguely industrial. I got a part-time teaching job at a
college an hour away, and commuted there twice a week.

Warren designed a line of ripstop nylon bags in vivid colors,
and continued to offer the old canvas ones, which seemed to look
forward to grime and mud stains. He undertook a catalog and, a
few years after that, began to sell on the Internet. As the years
passed, he became the first openly gay man in the Rotary Club,
then a member of the city council. He grew bald and his smile became creased like his father's. "I might run for Congress," Warren
said one morning.

"You don't mean that."

"I suppose not." Two years later he did mean it. The incumbent,
a charming homophobic conservative, was unbeatable, and nobody but Warren wanted to be the sacrificial Democrat. The business was doing well enough that we could put a little money into a
campaign managed by the husband of one of the Bettys. We received donations from distant gay organizations, and *All Things Considered* did a two-minute segment on Warren as part of a piece on
small-town gay candidates. Our big event was The Run for Congress, a ten-mile race that ended in front of Wanda's town hall. Warren, Glory, and I ran with a few supporters on a chilly fall day, and
to our chagrin, Warren's opponent entered the race and reached
the finish line before either of us. Warren lost the election more decisively than we expected. A few weeks later he began to talk about
leaving Wanda to study at Harvard for a year. "You're portable," he
said to me, as if I were my own laptop. "It's only a year."

"But we're happy here," I said, shocked. As we argued during the next months, he applied to a one-year "midcareer" master's program in government. "But why?" I kept asking.

"To meet people who aren't benighted. To see what comes next."

"Doesn't Bags of Wisconsin come next?"

"Maybe so, maybe not."

Many of my interviews had been with the benighted—that is, I'd noted homophobia, racism, or anti-Semitism—but each person I'd talked to, in conversations lasting so long that twilight fell, makeshift suppers intervened, or bars closed, was gradually revealed—somehow—to be decent and caring. My resistance to Warren increased; Wanda's very stop signs came to seem delicate with meaning. At first we argued, then we became silent or unpleasant. "Stay here, then," Warren said several times. One night in my helplessness I got so angry I took a swing at him. I didn't try to connect, but I knocked off his glasses, which snapped as they skittered across the floor. In his new glasses—much smaller lenses, with metal frames—Warren looked like someone else.

A few days later he said, "Don't you have a nephew in Boston? You can look up your nephew." Find another crazy Jew who bats his arms around, I thought he meant.

"Cousin," I said. Richard's nephew—his sister's son—lived near Boston. I stayed in touch with Richard, who was still a city planner in New York. Maybe he visited his nephew. Starting with Richard's image, I began to picture Cambridge bookstores and libraries, coffee shops where I could meet Richard or read galleys: the book on Wanda was almost done. I tried to stay civil as we rented out our house and put most of our furniture into storage. There was no way to take the oak desk, but I insisted on bringing the swivel armchair, which separated into a heavy base and a con-toured seat with a slatted back. I took a leave from my teaching job. In late June I drove east on Route 90 with middle-aged Glory in the backseat, catching sight now and then of a U-Haul truck driven by Warren.

The only apartment we could afford that would take a dog was in Somerville, the town next to Cambridge. People said Somerville was interesting, with the amenities that accompany graduate students and professional people when they move into a working-class town. But when I took Glory out to our small bare backyard, and waited, shovel in hand, until she squatted, I was aware only of what I didn't like: houses crowded together and cov-ered with aluminum siding, grassless yards, radios playing loud music. We ran on glaring sidewalks from which humid heat rose in visible waves. One day as I ran alone—Warren was in summer school, studying statistics and economics, scared and excited—an SUV hurtled down our steep, narrow street and struck a boy of ten or twelve sauntering across. He didn't fall down, and insisted when the driver jumped out that he was fine, man, fine. The kid and the van departed and I stood still, holding Glory's leash tightly and repelled by a place where everyone expected to inflict or receive pain. "Nonsense," said Warren that night. He was on his way out and he glanced back at me. "Brad, give it a rest, will you?"

After running, I'd shower and work on my copy editor's queries. Yes, the name "Burt"—Carroll Burt, a former mayor of Wanda—was spelled "Burtt" when it belonged to Carroll's un-cle, Landon. No, the Garfield family did not have two daughters named Mary Ellen. Warren took the T to Harvard Square, so I had the car, but I hated driving on the narrow streets. On good afternoons, Glory and I walked to Davis Square and I tied her up outside the used bookstore. I'd buy iced coffee and walk back with her, up and down hills, feeling a gingerly, grudging satisfaction.

The phone rang one dark fall afternoon when I'd postponed a walk too long. "Brad—Richard here—there's an incredible pianist performing with the symphony—" Richard said this into the machine because the phone had caught me on the toilet.

"I'm here," I said, picking up.

"Lucky boy! You escaped from the Midwest!"

"I like the Midwest." Richard was once a pianist. Wanda had no art, he had pointed out, on his single visit in the years we lived there. He discovered a French restaurant thirty miles away, but no music he'd sit still for. "Debussy," he was saying now. Richard was coming to Boston.

"I can't wait to see you," I broke in. "Warren and I are barely speaking."

"Oh, you and Warren are *fine*." Richard had never been with anyone long enough to consider living together, and regarded Warren and me as a couple comparable in dramatic potential to his parents. With a flurry of e-mailing and two more phone calls, Richard organized an evening. His nephew, Josh, was included, and so was Josh's girlfriend. "They live together," said Richard. "Right near you. She's Asian." Warren was too busy for Richard's concert, but I agreed to attend. Richard said I should pick up Josh and the woman, who had no car, and we'd all meet for dinner. "Can't we take the T?" I said.

"And you claim to resist city life!" said Richard. "No. The restaurant isn't near a station."

Josh—whom I'd met once or twice—was recognizably my relative: short, with curly hair and a brainy, Jewish look. He gave me directions from the passenger seat, while Jo, his tall girlfriend, asked self-assured questions behind me. She had long black hair and features I thought were Korean. Richard had told them about my books. "They sound intriguing," Jo said. "The little town in the Midwest—is that the latest one?"

"It's not out yet."

When I asked what she did, Jo said she worked in a day-care center. "I plan to quit just before I start wringing the necks of three-year-olds," she said. Then she said, "Maybe my book group will read your new book. We read and knit."

"My mother knitted," I said. Jo might be a tough critic, something like Richard's mother, my aunt Sylvia, who read my books and sent me long candid letters.

Richard waited—arms flung wide when he saw us—in one of his finds, an Italian restaurant in back of a deli. He squashed Josh in a hug, kissed me, and shook hands enthusiastically with Jo. "They have ostrich here. Order ostrich."

I ordered escarole-and-bean soup to start. As I tasted the soup, my mind was made to pay such close attention to my mouth (as escarole of just the right degree of doneness crossed my tongue) that everything became, with utter clarity, itself—as the soup was so precisely itself. My problem, I understood, wasn't Warren or Wanda or even my book, but solitude, because Warren—dear Warren—was all I had. We'd had friends in Wanda—good-hearted liberals who welcomed a gay couple—but I'd quickly forgotten them. The people I'd interviewed were make-believe friends.

When I paid attention again, Richard was quizzing Josh and Jo about Somerville. They'd just discussed movie houses and he was thoughtfully hearing their opinions of movies. Richard had been unhappy, I suspected, since he was drafted and sent to Vietnam, losing the chance for a life in music. He'd never loved anyone as he'd loved James, though he'd had a long line of young, self-absorbed boyfriends. But he could make any gathering festive, and discovered wonders of achievement and personality in those he met over dinner. I knew he delighted in treating his nephew, that he'd insist on paying for all of us—all of us kids. "So it's safe here at night? People walk around?" he asked now.

"Oh, sure," said Josh. "We walk everywhere."

I spoke of the SUV and the boy, the casual tolerance for mischance that I'd sensed, and Josh said, "Well, I didn't mean safe for pedestrians."

Then Jo said—and she sounded a little snippy, suddenly: "That's *not* what Brad meant."

"It's not?" said Josh.

"No. He meant people expect trouble here. Josh, you *know* it's not really safe."

"Oh," said Josh. "That."

"Yes. That."

"I didn't think you'd want to talk about it," he said.

"What?" Richard was saying. "Tell us the story. Is it gruesome?"

Jo looked around the table. I almost said, "Never mind." She drew a breath and said rapidly, "I was the last person at the day-care center one evening in March. While I was straightening up, a man came in and made me take off my clothes at knifepoint."

"Oh, my God," I said. Richard was silent.

Jo seemed to grow taller as she sat, twirling spaghetti on a fork. "He didn't touch me."

"That's supposed to make it all right?" I said.

"Well, some people say, 'Did he rape you?' and when I say no, they tell me about a friend somewhere who was raped."

"They didn't catch him?" said Richard.

Josh said, "I'm not sure the police took it seriously. They *said* they did."

"You mean they think something like that is normal here, nothing to get upset about?" I said.

"I don't know," said Josh. "All they've got is a description—just a nice-looking, middle-aged white guy."

"Maybe it was me," I said.

"Precisely," said Josh. "The thing is, something similar happened a couple more times, to different women."

"It was in the paper?" I said.

"Not that I know of," said Josh.

"Josh played detective," Jo said. "He's an idiot." We smiled, Richard and I, and she said, "It's not funny."

"She wants to be done with it," Josh said. "I respect that."

Our plates were cleared, and Richard looked at his watch. He'd come from the airport by taxi and now I'd drive everyone to Symphony Hall. While we waited for the check, Josh said he'd posted a notice on a few bulletin boards, giving an e-mail address. He wrote, "Recently my girlfriend was assaulted at her workplace by a white man of about fifty carrying a small black-handled knife.

Has anyone had a similar experience?" He'd received two replies. A secretary in a law firm in Medford, also the last person at closing time, had been ordered to undress by a "nice-looking" man in a baseball jacket, who fled when footsteps approached, just as she was starting to obey. And a graduate student had been drawn into conversation by a pleasant man who then led her at knifepoint into Powderhouse Park, but when he demanded that she undress she dropped what she was carrying and ran, and he didn't follow. She called the police, and someone went with her to collect her things, which were as she'd left them. Of course the man was nowhere around.

Richard insisted on paying, but the evening felt less festive, even tense, as we waited for him to receive his change. An old quarrel between Josh and Jo seemed to have been renewed, and it felt as if we'd violated Jo's privacy again just by hearing the story. I wanted to give her something in exchange, and so I contrived to tell my own story, which might seem as naked in its way as hers. "Richard, let me tell you what's been going on with me," I began, but then I turned toward Jo, explaining how we'd lived in Wanda, how Warren had made us move, and how—again, I suddenly understood something—we might never go back. I talked about our quarrels, even about the time I broke his glasses. I somehow worked in James, leaving Richard out of that story, of course. Meanwhile we left the restaurant and set out for Symphony Hall, and as I kept talking, I had a third realization. Now I explained as I drove, while Josh again directed me, that Wanda, for me, was the place where lovers did not die, where grief was cheated. Josh and Jo listened with, I sensed, nervous interest. They weren't used to stories about quarreling gay lovers, however firm their enlightened convictions might be. Quarreling gay lovers who were all but their uncles.

Richard was always right about music and I loved the concert with the dazzling pianist. At intermission Jo and Richard excused themselves and Josh and I were left in the old, grand auditorium, standing in the aisle near our seats. "Jo doesn't know this," Josh said, "but I'm meeting the two other women."

"Man, you're crazy," I said. "She's mad enough as things are."

"I have to."

"How did you arrange this?"

"I just told them who I was and set up a time and place. Maybe they won't come."

"What if Jo finds out?"

"She'll have to forgive me."

"All right," I said then, making up my mind to something— some act that would connect me to others. "I'm interested. Can I come along?"

He looked surprised. "Sure," he said. "I guess so." Jo was coming down the aisle. "I'll call you."

"Well, I'd like to," I said quietly.

That night I had more to tell Warren than he had to tell me, though I didn't tell him about the assault. I was feeling sheepish toward Warren, having had an inkling—several inklings—of why I'd resisted the move. I didn't want to tell him another, worse story about violence. It wasn't fair to claim that this was a menacing place. That driver had not expected to run down children on his way to work. The man with the knife was a troubled soul who might turn up in any town—in Wanda.

As I spoke, the small round glasses on Warren's broad face

flashed briefly in my direction. We sat in our living room—he in the single upholstered chair we'd brought, I in the oak armchair, with my fingers tracing the familiar grain of the wood—and Warren stared tiredly past me at one of our few pieces of art, a poster announcing a show of Chinese painting. It depicted a scene from a scroll on which small people trekked over detailed stretches of mountain. Sometimes in my working day I looked at it, and it made me sad to think of the trip they still had ahead of them, which I could see though they couldn't. Warren began to talk about one of his classes. A woman had made a presentation about decisions she'd made when running a small family business.

"Useful for when we get back to Wanda," I said. "What kind of business?"

"It failed. Something to do with software," he said. "*If* we get back to Wanda."

I was as shocked as if I hadn't had my string of epiphanies that evening. "Betty can't run that business forever," I said.

"I could sell it," said Warren.

I was silent, and as I sat looking at my own spot on the opposite wall—which was bare—Glory gave off a weary German shepherd noise, then stretched and walked toward the back door, her claws clicking on the bare wood floor. I followed her, reaching for my coat.

Josh had told the graduate student and the secretary he'd carry a green backpack and wear a red watch cap, and they both came to the coffeehouse he'd specified. It was a cold day, and shrugging off coats, everyone seemed pleased to be indoors. The student had brought her roommate, and the secretary—who talked with a Boston accent—had brought her brother, a man bursting out of his clothes, who I thought might be a plainclothes cop. He wouldn't have coffee, just water. *"A glass of water,"* he said pointedly. "Not water you pay for, in a bottle." He said "bawdle." Josh bought coffee for the women and himself and asked for a glass of water. I bought my own coffee, then helped him carry everything. He was fluttery.

Immediately the women told each other their stories. They were instantly comfortable, though one, who I thought had never been in this coffee shop, was probably from an Italian family that was gradually being priced out of Somerville by the arrival of people like the other, who might have come often to sit in a dim corner with a laptop.

"I should have walked faster and gotten away," said the student, "but he seemed harmless. I wasn't positive I didn't know him."

"You thought you knew him?" said Josh.

"You know how it is when somebody speaks to you, and you're not sure if he's a stranger, or someone you've met before?"

"Same here," said the secretary. "I was embarrassed that I didn't recognize him. I thought he was a lawyer."

Josh had put the green backpack on the table and as he listened he played with the cinch cord that closed the main compartment, pressing and releasing the toggle, then twisting the black elastic around his fingers and letting it untwist. Bags of Wisconsin offered sturdier backpacks, and our cinch cords didn't get as stretched and frayed as Josh's was. "We could talk about what the guy looked like," he said rapidly. "My girlfriend couldn't come, but I know what she remembers. And we could chart the places where this happened."

He took a notebook from his pack, tore out a sheet of lined paper, and began drawing a map, just indicating main streets. It was difficult, and he turned the paper over and tried again, while everyone watched patiently. The angles were surely wrong in the second map as well—Somerville has few right angles—but the map made clear what we already knew: the man had operated in an area about a mile wide. As Josh worked, Marie, the secretary, said, "His hair was beginning to get gray, little flecks all over his head."

"I didn't see any gray," said Sarah, the grad student.

"My girlfriend said light brown hair," Josh said.

"Maybe it's not the same man," I put in.

"You think there are *two*?" said the brother. It was the first time he'd spoken since he asked for the water, which he had drunk in a few gulps, squashing the tall paper cup when he was done.

"I guess not," I said.

When Josh suggested that we three men stand, the women agreed that the man was taller than Josh or me, and possibly a little taller than Marie's brother. "I'm five-nine," said the brother. There was something touching about all this. It felt like being in a boys' book, but the boys would solve the crime and we wouldn't.

At this point Sarah's roommate, who'd said her name was Francesca, spoke to me. "Could you tell me your interest in all this? Why are you here?"

"He's my cousin," said Josh.

"I asked to come," I said. "I just moved here."

"How come? Work?" Francesca continued.

"My partner's in grad school."

"And what do you do?"

"I'm a writer," I said reluctantly.

"For a magazine?" she said. "I sort of thought you might be. And if you're thinking of writing a story about all this, well, I don't know—" She looked at Sarah.

So I told them what I wrote. "I suppose I could write about Somerville next," I said, "but it's probably been done."

Francesca seemed satisfied, and what I'd said seemed to make it possible for others to change the subject or leave. Sarah said she had a class, and Josh looked at his watch and hurried away, too. Nothing tangible had come of the meeting. Marie and her brother had a car parked nearby, so that left Francesca and me, and we stepped out together into the wind. We were going in different directions, but we crossed two streets in Davis Square before separating, and as we walked, Francesca said, "Frankly, I want this thing to get all the publicity possible, if only Sarah's name isn't in it. She was sure the police thought she made it up, and sometimes she thinks she imagined it, but of course she didn't."

"Of course not."

"I'm going to tell you something," Francesca said. "You can do what you want with it. The man's name is probably Randall Strout. He's also a writer. Maybe you've come across him."

Of course I was astonished. She was turning away. "But you have to tell me how you know," I said. "And why you aren't telling."

"I know because Sarah did recognize him, but she doubts herself. She'd met him at a party a few weeks earlier. She was pretty sure it was the same man when he talked to her that night—that's why she was friendly. Later she began to wonder. And she doesn't want to accuse anybody if he isn't—oh, you get the picture."

"But you're sure?" I said.

"Sarah doesn't hallucinate," Francesca said. "I'm freezing. I have to go."

A few days later, I looked up Randall Strout on the Internet, feeling uncomfortable as I did it. Francesca believed Sarah but I thought Sarah probably distrusted herself with good reason, and what I was doing seemed like spreading a false rumor, even if I told nobody why I typed the name I did into my search engine. I probably did it not because I was so interested in Josh's pursuit of the criminal but because I was looking for something to do. I'd had a few freelance editing projects, but my main task right now, with my book in production, was to find the subject of my next book. I was happy on the days I wandered around Boston, learning random facts in the hope that one of them would start a succession of thoughts, but the cold deterred me, and too often I stayed in the apartment with Glory. We had brought so few books that I couldn't even waste a day reading. Talking to local writers, or reading them, might be a plausible way to begin, but this was a funny way to find local writers. Randall Strout, it turned out, had written two books, both out of print. The more recent one was about the politics behind the redevelopment of the Boston North End and the construction of the Faneuil Hall market and Lewis Wharf; the other, written long ago, was a memoir called *Boy in Winter*. He taught at a college in a Boston suburb. He was I, in other words—a slightly less lucky version of me, since one of my old books was still in print. Still feeling odd, I let myself look in used bookstores for works by Randall Strout, and my heart pounded when I found the one about politics. I bought it, then read a chapter or two. It wasn't bad, and wasn't completely different from a book I might write, except that it looked less at individuals and more at the workings of government. I left it around and Warren picked it up. "You're starting to think of local topics," he said. "I told you."

One day I found myself reading the phone book, one of the few books we had. Then it occurred to me to look up Randall Strout—and yes, he lived not far away, and yes, after doing something else for an hour, I called him. If he had answered, I might have hung up, but when I got a message ("Randy and Ann are out, but—") I left a message on his answering machine, identifying myself, saying I'd come across his book, that I had written comparable books and was new in town, that I wondered if we might meet. I had no trouble telling the partial truths I told. When I hung up I no longer felt strange. It seemed simply absurd—a fantasy of the young—to think this writer with a friendly voice and a wife named Ann was a criminal, an example of a deplorable person in a book he or I might write. I was annoyed with Francesca on Randall Strout's behalf and on mine.

Randall Strout phoned me, and I walked through light snow to meet him at a coffee shop—a different one. His photograph on the book jacket was blurry and out-of-date, but I recognized him. He was my age or older, with a friendly, open face. His hair looked evenly brown, with no gray.

"Randy Strout," he said, rising, extending his hand, when I approached.

"Brad Kaplowitz." I took off my gloves to shake his hand.

"I like this place. Good choice," he said. He had a cup of coffee in front of him, and I soon returned with my own. Before long we were jumping from topic to topic. We knew people who'd worked with each other's agents or editors, we'd published in the same magazines. He told me about his divorce, and his new wife and small daughter.

"You have kids?" he asked, and I shook my head, then explained what I was doing in the Boston area and with whom. "So how d'you feel," he said, "plucked out of your life like that?"

"Oh, this might be a better life. I don't know many writers in Wisconsin."

"Still," he said.

I resisted a little longer. "It made sense for my partner."

"But you didn't bring your books, did you?"

"No," I admitted. "Sometimes I read the phone book. That's how I found you." I told him about Wanda, about Warren's parents, about Bags of Wisconsin—and even something about my earlier life in New York. I heard myself talk too long, and swallowed the last of my coffee. "I should go."

"I have your phone number," he said, rising, "and you have mine." I didn't think I'd call him again. I liked him too much. I don't mean I was attracted, not at all, but it made me uncomfortable, after all, to think of him as a possible friend, when I'd heard of him in such a strange way. I couldn't call Francesca, whose last name I didn't know, but I badly wanted to tell her, "It's not the same man." Yet I knew that even if I could reach her I couldn't say it, because I didn't know it. As we stepped from the coffee shop, I turned to Randy to shake hands again. The snow had stopped and sunlight gleamed through clouds. I saw in the light that his hair was flecked with gray.

In the next weeks I finished one editing job and was occupied with another, more lucrative one that bored me. I minded the cold weather more than I did in Wisconsin, for some reason, and often didn't go outside. In January Warren had begun new courses, and now he worked late, often in our living room, on a negotiation project with three other students, who pretended to be bureaucrats in the fictional town of Dalrymple, which was being choked by pollution coming from Dunbar, upriver and upwind of them. Dunbar was a working-class town with a paper mill, Dalrymple an affluent suburb.

Sometimes I'd go in and argue—a scarf around my neck because the apartment was poorly insulated—taking the side of Dunbar. I imagined factory workers and lumbermen struggling against these Harvard intellectuals, though of course the Dunbar team was played by four other students. After the rest of his team left, I'd rouse myself to fight with Warren. Whatever he said, I'd oppose it. When I wasn't siding with Dunbar against Dalrymple, I was siding with the three others on his team against him. I watched myself make foolish arguments, just to upset him. I wanted him to seize me and hurt me or make love to me—make love to me violently—but when we did make love, now and then, it was perfunctory, a reasonable accommodation to our physical needs.

One day Josh phoned. "I'm taking advantage of your good nature and your status as my first cousin once removed," he said. He wanted to buy a bookcase and wondered if I'd help him carry it home in my car. The following Saturday it had snowed again, but I dug the car out and drove Josh to a furniture store in Central Square, needing only a little help finding my way. He chose an unpainted pine bookcase.

"How's Jo?" I said as we waited for the clerk to ring it up.

"Fine," he said. "I finally told her about that meeting."

"Was she mad?"

"I think she was mad that I didn't include her, but she couldn't say that, it would be so inconsistent. I've lost interest, anyway. It's almost a year. I guess he wasn't a serial killer."

We lifted the bookcase over the packed snow and eased it into the backseat of my car, then found a hardware store so Josh could buy sandpaper, brushes, and red paint. I offered to help him get started, and we went to his apartment.

Jo was out, and by the time she arrived, Josh and I had finished sanding the bookcase. She looked amused at our project (*"Red?"* she said). She left the room, then returned. I was telling Josh about Warren and the negotiating team, and he was telling me he wanted to apply to graduate school someday, if he only knew in what, and only had the money.

"I hear you participated in Josh's tea party with crime victims, Brad," Jo said, behind me. She spoke with cool irony, like a much older woman.

"Do I owe you an apology?" I said.

"It's not you who owes me an apology," Jo said, "but I've more or less had it. I might have liked to be there—if I could have been invisible."

I said, "We could have arranged to have you typing on a laptop behind us. You could have taken notes."

"I hope you didn't speak loudly enough to be heard," Jo said severely, flinging her long hair over her shoulder.

"I wish I'd told you," said Josh. "It would have made you feel better, just to talk to those women."

"Yeah, but I was the only one stupid enough to actually disrobe. That would make me feel great," Jo said. "That would have made me feel stunningly perverted."

There was silence as Josh applied paint to the underside of a shelf.

Then I said, "Jo, if you knew who the man was, would you press charges?"

"No," she said quickly. "I just couldn't. And I don't need some lawyer trying to make me feel like a whore."

Josh looked up at her from his knees, his hair spattered with red paint. "You *mean* that?" he said. "Don't you think this guy needs to be stopped?"

"Yes," Jo said, looking down at him. "But not by me. And anyway, I don't want him locked up for twenty years followed by having to register as a sexual predator everywhere he goes—I just want him to quit it."

"Does that jibe with your deepest principles?" pursued Josh. He was holding the paintbrush at an angle, and it was dripping on the floor, just beyond the newspaper.

"No," said Jo steadily. "In this instance, I am not capable of living according to my principles. I mean"—and for a moment she sounded less grown-up, even childish—"if it came up—if you found the nice-looking middle-aged man with the black-handled hunting knife—I wouldn't be."

A few weeks later, it was lighter in the late afternoons, though no warmer. Warren had begun to talk about looking for a job in Boston. I watched myself, waiting to see if I was going to fight him, leave him and return to Wanda alone, or look for a teaching job myself. Then one afternoon, Randy Strout called me. "I came across something I want to give you," he said. "May I stop by with it? Where do you live?"

His friendliness was irresistible. I'd had a difficult day: errands in the cold and pointless Web surfing, instead of exercise and work. A few days earlier, I'd mentioned the idea of a book on Somerville to my editor, who dismissed it with disconcerting promptness. "Too local," she said.

"What could be more local than Wanda, Wisconsin?"

"Wanda, Wisconsin, is so local it's universal."

That book would be out soon. She was vague about promotion.

Now I said to Randy, "Give me twenty minutes," told him where I lived—with only an instant's hesitation—and straightened up a little. I was pleased to have any visitor.

A little while later the doorbell rang, and I could see Randy's genial face above his blue parka through the small dirty window in our front door. He was holding something. I hurried to let him in while Glory barked. Randy stepped back warily, but I took her firmly by the collar. "She won't bother you." Before taking off his jacket, he waved a magazine at me. "I bet you haven't seen this." Wouldn't you know, the man subscribed to *Publishers Weekly*. He'd been the first to spot the review of my book about Wanda. The magazine was open to the page, and he thrust it under my chin. "Oh, my God," I said. I took it and read it. It was good.

"I bought something to celebrate," he said. He had a small bakery box, the kind I remembered from boyhood, tied with string. I led him into our tiny kitchen, with Glory following, her tail swinging. I made coffee. He took off his parka and arranged it on the back of his chair. Again we were full of talk. The man liked

I put it into my pocket. My half of the brownie was still in the box. I threw it away and washed the cups. Then I called Richard at his office in New York, and told him what I'd done. He listened without comment, except for a long exhalation of breath. Then came an extended pause. "Did you tell him to get help, to see someone?"

"No."

"Did you keep the knife?"

"No."

Another pause, and he began to talk about a second concert he thought he might come to in Boston. "I'll be in touch." Then he said, "Who else are you going to tell?"

"I have to tell Jo," I said. "Jo and Josh. Warren."

I got off the phone and went searching for Jo and Josh's phone number, looking in my agitation in all the wrong places. I looked again. I still couldn't find it. I sat down in Warren's oak chair and held on to the arms. Anger, I saw—this time the discovery counted—had waited for me all my life.

Pastries at the Bus Stop

As I told my sister later, any reasonable person would have made the same remark. I was standing at a bus stop on Madison Avenue when a woman came out of a bakery carrying a little wooden table. She put it down near the curb and went back inside. Then she brought out a tray of French pastries: the chocolate was dark and glossy, the glazed strawberries fat, the crusts flaky. Whipped cream swirled and swooped. The woman set the tray on the table, right in front of me. She opened the rear doors of a van that was illegally parked in the bus stop, slowly slid the tray inside, shut the doors, and carried the table back into the store. I looked around, and saw nobody but an old man walking a brown dog. I said to him, "Did you see that tray? Makes you want to rush to a hotel and go to bed, doesn't it?"

"You *didn't*," said Ruth, when I told her about it.

"I did."

"You went to a hotel?"

"Oh, no, he probably didn't even hear me. But I did say it. I—"

My sister yelled, but my point was that I had changed. My reason for speaking, and for telling Ruth about it, was not to bring humiliation and pain on my head, as it would have been not so many years earlier. I said it—and I described saying it—to celebrate the sexiness of French pastries at the bus stop. Ruth and I were meeting at Bloomingdale's to pick out a dress for her to be married in, and the wedding was five days off. I wouldn't have gone to a hotel with the man walking the dog, even if he'd been attractive, had wanted to, and wasn't accompanied by his dog, because Ruth urgently needed a wedding dress. Also, I had an appointment later with the man I loved.

The bus arrived as the woman came rushing out of the store again, waving car keys apologetically. And then life became a little complicated, because as I got on the bus my cell phone rang. I was the director of an organization with the innocent name of Neighborhood Helpers, and the caller was my assistant, Georgiana, who was still at our office downtown, where she'd received a phone call from a client's daughter. We were a nonprofit agency—so nonprofit we were always about to go out of business for lack of money to buy a new ink cartridge for the printer. We placed ex-crazies, ex-junkies, and reformed alcoholics—sometimes known as psychiatric survivors and recovering substance abusers—in part-time jobs assisting old people, and then we kept track of everybody while the old people's lightbulbs were changed, their library books returned, or their bathrooms cleaned. Our goal was to stay out of the papers except for one schmaltzy story every year. That wasn't too hard: we picked our employees carefully, and I could give you pages of statistics on the rarity of violence among former drinkers, drug users, and mental patients. The greatest risk, ordinarily, was that a recovering addict would bore an old lady to death explaining the more obscure steps of a twelve-step program. A typical newspaper story showed a tall, shy depressive taking a box of cornflakes off the top shelf in the supermarket for a smiling old woman leaning on a walker, but now and then people's peculiarities coincided in some unpredictable way and an obsessive-compulsive who spent her days washing her hands was paired with an early-stage Alzheimer's victim who couldn't remember whether he'd washed his hands that week. So I worried because Georgiana, when she called me, sounded worried. The client was Mrs. Cohen, a diabetic who injected herself with insulin. Mrs. Cohen's daughter had said her mother was now too confused to do this properly, and our worker had provided more help than the daughter considered acceptable.

"Who's the worker?" I asked Georgiana.

"Bernadette." Bernadette was an ex-junkie who maybe knew too much about needles.

"I'll talk to Bernie tomorrow," I said. I got off the bus and walked over to Bloomingdale's. "Wedding-dress time!" I greeted Ruth.

"*Please* let's not call it a wedding dress," she said. "That's what Mom keeps saying—wedding dress. Mom's being impossible." Ruth was almost sixty and it was a second marriage for both her and the man, whose name was Bob and who had a number of rough little places in his personality upon which Ruthie seemed to thrive. They chewed on each other like people who grab the crustiest part of the turkey skin at Thanksgiving dinner. "And let's get coffee first," Ruth said.

"Okay," I said. "Coffee. But then we're buying a dress. Not a wedding dress, all right, but a *nice dress.*" While Ruth and I had coffee I told her about the pastries at the bus stop and she yelled. Ruth's usual take on me was that despite marked improvements (no suicide attempts in many years, useful employment, a cat who was up to date with all his shots) I was still self-destructive and the main way to tell was that the man I loved was married. Then I told her about the woman who'd called about Bernie, and Ruth objected some more. "You're asking for trouble, sending these people into apartments unsupervised."

"When we started," I said, "the employee and the client met at the senior center and went shopping, but the old people started sneaking them home."

"And now your worker's sticking needles into somebody. Needles!"

"I'm sure it's fine," I said. I said that Bernie had been clean for three years, was taking community college courses, and had all but managed to get her kids out of foster care.

"I'm in a funny mood," said Ruth, putting down her cup.

We picked out a blue silk calf-length dress with long sleeves. "I'm not telling you to become *respectable,*" she said in the dressing room, slithering into it. Ruthie had long tangled gray hair and she was shedding on the new dress, even before she had it on. "I hate *'respectable.'*" She spoke while it was bunched over her head and I had trouble making out what she was saying.

"I know," I said. The dress looked good.

"Can I walk in it?" she asked.

"You don't need to walk in it."

"I walk in everything." It had a slit up one side, so she could

walk in it, she demonstrated, squashing me against the mirror as she took an exaggerated long stride across the dressing room. I put my arms around her and held tight, wondering if it would be harder to see her alone once she was married, though she and Bob already lived together and I seemed to be seeing her now. I'd never been married, and she'd been divorced for years and years.

Ruth paid for the dress and said she was going back to her office—she was a magazine editor—though it was past six. As we were standing in the street outside the store, about to go in separate directions, she started to cry. I put my hands on her shoulders. "What?" I said.

"I don't like the dress," said Ruth.

"Are you sure?" I said.

"No." Then she said, "Let's rent a car and drive to California."

"You'd want to take Bob along."

"I don't need him," said Ruth. She was joking but tears were sliding down her face. I patted her arms and let her go.

"And I don't need Mom and Dad showing up," she said. In their late eighties, our parents still lived independently and could fly up from Florida for a wedding. For years in my difficult twenties and thirties I didn't talk to them, as I made my way in and out of emergency rooms, psychiatric hospitals, and day programs. When I let them call me again I had had a long enough vacation, and their peculiarities bothered me less than they bothered Ruth, who'd been dealing with them all along. Our parents seemed sweet and frail to me, passive-aggressive and exhaustingly anxious to her.

"I'm late," I said. The man I loved was named Brian, and we were meeting downtown. Though Brian and I ate dinner and performed ordinary sex as well, we called our evenings oral-sex dates because I loved to be licked. Some guys will, some won't, but he loved it, too, and his wife didn't. All I could think of was my mouth by the time I saw him, my mouth and his mouth. We met at a little restaurant on Second Avenue, ate paella with mussels and clams—which seemed like a rehearsal—then took a taxi to my place on the Lower East Side. I told people I lived in the building where my grandparents lived when they came to America, though I had no idea where they lived.

It was fall, cold out, and Brian and I were chilled. We hurried into bed, dislodging my cat, and pressed our hands together, then ran them up and down each other's legs and arms and buttocks and back, swiftly and roughly, to get warm. Brian not only liked licking, he liked fat women, and I was one; his wife had been fat but had lost weight. Once we were warm and laughing we got to the business of mouths.

"My sister's getting married on Sunday," I said sometime later.

"And you're upset that you can't invite me," he said.

"No," I said. "I'm looking forward to seeing family. It'll be easier, not having to look after a date."

"That's healthy of you."

"I'm healthy." I thought for a while and said, "But ordinarily you'd be right."

"About what?"

"Women who date married men hate it that they can't take them places," I said. "You knew right away because you've had quite a bit of experience with single women."

"Is that a disqualification?" he said.

"No," I said. We'd been dating for a year and I had a pretty good idea of his history. I thought for a long time, and something kept me from just moving on to another topic. It was something about the way he'd said, "Is that a disqualification?" What it meant was fine, but not the way he said it. It was weary, as if he'd known something for a while that I resisted knowing. I said, "But if you've done it so many times, why did you stop? What happened to them? Why aren't you in bed with one of them right this minute?"

"Sometimes they ended it, sometimes I did," he said. "Isn't that how it's been for you?" He was quiet for a moment. "Sometimes it's time to behave for a while."

I thought about what behaving might mean for him. "I see," I said, and touched him again, and he responded.

Next morning when I arrived at the office, a former Chinese take-out place that always smelled of cooking oil, Georgiana— a light-skinned black woman with formidable multitudes of braids—was listening to one of the employees, Jerry, a Vietnam vet. "So I says to him," Jerry was saying, "because he can't seem to hear me, Pete, you wearing your hearing aids? And he says, What? And I go, Your *hearing* aids, and he goes, What? and I go HEARING AIDS and he still doesn't get it, so I say, The things . . . you use . . . to help . . . you *hear*. And he says, Oh, my *hearing* aids, sure, I'm wearing 'em."

Georgiana shook her head and we laughed, and then Mrs. Cohen's daughter phoned, just as I was thinking what a fine, friendly little project we ran. As we spoke I looked at a map of downtown Manhattan over Georgiana's desk. We put pushpins where we had clients. Each worker was supposed to have a different color pushpin, but there were more employees than colors, and Georgiana didn't bother to keep the map up-to-date. Still, it looked impressive, and I liked staring at it while I talked on the phone. At first I didn't mind talking to this daughter, who seemed to find her mother dear if exasperating. We laughed together; then she got more specific. Mrs. Cohen had injected herself with insulin for years, until her daughter had found a syringe on the floor and called in visiting nurses. But for some reason, Medicare had stopped paying for the nurses, and the daughter was glad, because she wanted her mother to move into assisted living. Once the nurses were canceled, the mother agreed to go, but Bernadette was spoiling the plan by reeducating Mrs. Cohen about injections—or doing the injecting herself.

"We're talking about needles," said the daughter, sounding like my sister. "We're talking about practicing medicine without a license."

"Well . . ." I said.

"I am a physician," said the daughter. She'd chosen the right moment to say that, like a pilot choosing the right moment to push a button and bomb a picturesque village out of existence.

"I'll talk to Bernadette," I said.

"Do more than talk," she said. "I'm sorry. I know this Bernadette person means well."

I was about to try to reach Bernie when the phone rang again, and it was Ruth. "I took back the dress," she said.

"Why did you do *that*?"

"It was too appropriate," she said. "If I have to get married with a rabbi and all my relatives, at least I want to look inappropriate."

I wrote "Bernadette" on a pad in front of me, and underlined it twice. I said, "It wasn't white with a veil."

"Still. But you're right—Bob says I'm crazy."

"And didn't you tell me this is an extremely casual rabbi?" I said.

"Yes. A woman." Ruth and I are Jewish—and so is Bob—but you'd never know it from anything we do, although I suppose you'd know it from what we think. Ruth's daughter had found this rabbi. "I don't dress up," said Ruth. "I don't stand up before clergy."

"You could change," I said, becoming annoyed. I needed to call Bernie. "You've never been a complete mess, so you've never had to change. It would do you good to change, for once. I've changed so many times."

"I wouldn't change in *that* direction," said Ruth.

Then I noticed Bernadette herself, standing next to the mailboxes near the front door. Bernie was a tall, grandly proportioned woman who weighed a lot but looked great. She was glancing at some papers with her coat on. "I have to hang up," I said to Ruth. I put down the receiver and chased Bernie.

"Hey, Lilly," she greeted me.

"You practicing medicine without a license?" I said.

"Cohen's daughter?"

"Cohen's *doctor* daughter."

"Nobody knows more than I do about injections," Bernie said. She got taller as we stood there.

We took the bus to Mrs. Cohen's apartment. Taking up most of the aisle, Bernie talked loudly about her kids. "I wasn't the best mother," she said, "but I wasn't the worst. We had TV rules. We had sugar rules."

When Mrs. Cohen came to the door, she looked better than some. She had white hair twisted on top of her head, more like my dead grandmother's than my mother's bleached blond waves. Mrs. Cohen's bun was not straight, but it was firmly hairpinned, and her eyes were dark and sharp. She wore a black sweatshirt with dandruff on it. Bernie beamed down at her. "I brought my boss," she said.

"You don't look like a boss," said Mrs. Cohen. "You look like my daughter."

"I understand your daughter is a doctor," I said loudly and slowly, but Mrs. Cohen could hear.

"A psychiatrist," she said. Over the years I've had a few good encounters with psychiatrists, but enough bad ones that I'd have preferred her daughter to be a dermatologist. Then she asked, "Do you pay a decent wage?"

"An old leftie?" I said.

"I never joined the Party," said Mrs. Cohen.

"She tells me about those times," Bernie said. "She went to jail."

The apartment was not too messy, except for a frying pan on the sofa. "So, honey, how's your sugar?" said Bernie.

Mrs. Cohen glanced at me, and I saw that she was prepared to lie about what they'd been up to, but Bernie was too proud. She showed me how she'd arranged the paraphernalia of diabetes—the little device to prick Mrs. Cohen's finger, the glucometer, the book in which to record blood sugar readings, then the insulin in its labeled jars in the refrigerator, and the syringes. "The used ones we put in here," said Bernie, patting a coffee can. She'd been coming twice a day, every day, though she was paid to come only once and not on weekends. They showed me their routine. Bernie handed Mrs. Cohen each thing she needed. "We take it nice and slow," she said.

Their intent faces—old and young, white and black—were as beautiful in an even better way than the pastries at the bus stop. I didn't know what to say. "How long have you lived here, Mrs. Cohen?" I asked.

"My daughter thinks I don't take baths," she said. I had noticed a whiff of not-quite-enough-baths.

"We can do baths," said Bernie.

On our way out of the building, I said to my employee, "You're not being paid for most of this. What do you get out of it?"

"You need to ask?" Bernie said, and in truth I didn't. "Mrs. Cohen says I'm *right*," she said. "She says the government takes people's kids for no reason, and black people don't get a fair deal. She tells me that every day. That's what I get."

"I see what you mean," I said.

"She really was a Communist," said Bernie. "She wouldn't tell you, because you're the boss."

We separated outside. Probably Bernadette would walk around the block, go back inside, and have additional conspiracies with Mrs. Cohen, and I didn't care. It was a warm day and the office wasn't far, so I decided to walk, but first I went into a coffee shop and ordered a cappuccino, and while I drank it, an impulse made me call Brian at work, something I hardly ever did. I felt like talking about my life—about Ruth's exasperating behavior over the wedding dress, about Mrs. Cohen and her daughter and Bernie. But of course he was preoccupied at work, and I became self-conscious. After barely mentioning Bernie and Mrs. Cohen, and leaving Ruth out, I said what I suppose I had called to say: "Was there something else you wanted to say last night?"

He sighed. "No," he said. Long pause. Then, "Not now. But maybe in a couple of weeks, yes."

"I get it," I said, and hung up. I thought, *But I love him!* By which I meant, I think, not just that I could talk to him as well as fuck him, and not, on the other hand, that I was prepared to nurse him through cancer or whatever his wife might have agreed to undertake as part of her marriage vows. I meant that for me, losing him would be a disaster. I wished I hadn't called, but what can you do? I finished my cappuccino and walked back to the office. On the way I came to a jewelry store, and I bought a ruby pendant on a thick silver chain. When you've had as much training in low times as I have, you know when to buy something quickly. I was wearing a black V-necked sweater and the pendant hung just above my breasts, looking lovely on my skin. The ruby was mounted in silver with an elaborate, old-fashioned design. I didn't wear the necklace out of the store. I clutched the silver-and-ruby pendant in my hand, and twisted the cord around my fingers. I needed something in my hand.

"I believe in change," I said to Bernie the next day. "I above all people believe in change. I'm different from the way I was, you're different from the way you were. I'm not sure Mrs. Cohen can become different. Can become better."

"You white folks," Bernie said. "You lock away your grandmas. I wouldn't lock my grandma away."

"The assisted living place is not a prison," I said.

"What's the worst that can happen?" said Bernie. "She'll die? She's *gonna* die."

"I know."

Ruth called me late that night. "I had a fight with Mom on the phone," she said. "She wants me to go back and buy the dress again. Could you tell her there was something wrong with it?"

"You're sixty years old," I said. "What do you care what Mom thinks?"

"Fifty-nine," she said. "I'm going to wear woolen pants and a silk jacket. Silk is dressy. I forgot I had it."

"What color?" I asked.

"Black."

"Well, you didn't want to be appropriate. Just don't ask me to explain it to Mom."

"Are you okay?" she said then. I'd been crying just before she called.

"Brian's getting ready to dump me," I said.

"Oh, Lilly," she said. "Oh, Lilly, honey."

"Well, right," I said. Then I brought her up-to-date on Mrs. Cohen.

"What will you do?" she said. "You'll have to fire Bernie. At least reassign her."

"I would never fire Bernie!" I said. "I thought you didn't believe in appropriate. I thought you didn't believe in respectable."

"Lilly, you don't need this daughter as your enemy."

"You think it's okay to be outrageous," I said, "but only if nobody's heart gets broken."

I didn't fire Bernie, or reassign her. I told her to visit Mrs. Cohen only when she was being paid for it and to stay away from the diabetes equipment.

"But she'll make a mistake," said Bernie.

"I thought you taught her so well she won't make a mistake."

"She's an old lady!" Bernie shouted. We were standing near the mailboxes, and people were listening. I didn't argue. Two weeks after Ruth's wedding, Mrs. Cohen's daughter found Bernie injecting her mother, and eventually she did close us down—or, something closed us down—but it took a long time. Possibly we kept going longer than we would have, because the bad publicity attracted some donations. And at around the same time, Brian did regretfully hint at some difficulties his wife was going through, which required his more scrupulous presence.

The night before the wedding, I took my parents out to dinner. They were tired from the flight, a little trembly. They seemed smaller than when I'd seen them last. My mother said I definitely should have gotten a haircut for the wedding, while my father said he hoped I wasn't going to wear high heels, in which I could tear a ligament and be laid up for weeks if not months. I couldn't tell them about Brian, but I told the story of Mrs. Cohen and Bernie. My father, to my surprise, thought I did right not to reassign Bernie. My mother said my father and I were both crazy.

When I dressed for Ruth's wedding the next day—in a tight pink silk dress with matching heels, and with the ruby around my neck—I could predict some of my future pretty accurately, but I was excited about the party, and the people I'd see. The wedding was in a private room in a restaurant, with thick gray carpet and blue drapes and chairs. It was just as well that Ruth had returned the dress—she'd have matched the decor. Ruthie's hair was pinned up like Mrs. Cohen's and she looked not exactly inappropriate but terribly serious in her black silk jacket—shy and cute. She'd told me to come early, and when I arrived we hugged. "You look like the bride," she said.

"Somebody had to."

When I was young, I attempted suicide thirteen times. Now I don't see my life in contrast to the lives of other women my age, with their marriages, their children. My life contrasts with my death, and at times everything seems to have sharp edges, as if the people I know—work people, family, friends and lovers—were cutouts, not paper dolls but dolls made of metal. They are so real they seem not quite alive, for a moment, and when I touch their edges electricity sparks. They are so real it is a painful joy to be near them, no matter what they are like as people. The room began to fill. Ruth's daughter came in, weepy. Then her son, David, arrived grinning, bringing our parents. Ruth put her hands on our father's ears when she saw him, and pretended to pull them. His ears stuck out in a funny way, and Ruth always teased him. Bob, the groom, came—a kind, strong-looking man in an ill-fitting suit—moving that day with a look of slow surprise. He came with a brother who looked like him, and a daughter, a tall midwife named Binnie, who once dated—maybe even lived with—Ruth's son. My cousin Joan, a psychologist, came over and demanded to know what I'm up to—apparently surprised to see me alive—and reintroduced me to her son, whom I'd last seen as a little kid. Now he had an impressive-looking Asian wife or girlfriend. But before Joan and I could speak, there was a stir, and it was Joan's mother, Aunt Sylvia, arriving, brought by her son, my cousin Richard. Richard was *old,* I noticed, the first of the cousins to be old, but Aunt Sylvia, who was truly old, just looked like Aunt Sylvia. My aunt had short white hair, a hooked Jewish nose, and a loud, clear voice. She and my mother were the last alive of six siblings. I don't know how long it had been since they'd seen each other. Richard steered Aunt Sylvia into the room carefully, because she was blind. My mother turned at the commotion and stepped forward, blond and wrinkled, her arms lifted unsteadily.

"Fanny!" shouted Sylvia, blind though she was, and Mom called, "Sylvia darling!" Sylvia had a cane, but she took long steps, leaving Richard behind. She and my mother embraced in the center of the room, while everyone clapped.

A chuppah was set up in a corner. Chairs were brought for the old people, and the rest of us gathered. The rabbi performed the ceremony. Everyone said "Mazel tov" and wept a little. Waiters brought food. I was moving toward the bar when a man I hadn't recognized called, "Lilly, Lilly!" and it was my cousin Bradley, now a writer in Boston, a gay man already in his fifties, though I used to consider him a baby. "We have to talk," said Bradley—Brad, he's called now—who was my favorite when he was six, with more hair, and I was nine. We walked to the bar and he asked for a glass of white wine. On antidepressants you have to be careful, so I postponed my single drink. "I'll just have a glass of water," I said to the bartender.

"Ice?"

"Mmm."

Brad and I clinked glasses, and I sipped. In an hour I'd get my Chardonnay. "Are you happy?" I asked my cousin.

He smiled. "Are you?"

"I know," I said. "What a question."

The Odds It Would Be You

In 1976, when Bradley Kaplowitz was twenty-eight, he took lessons and learned to drive. A New Yorker with a pocket full of subway tokens costing fifty cents each, he rented a Dodge Dart so he could take his bald mother, Bobbie, on vacation. Bradley worked at a downtown bookstore, where a regular customer had mentioned an old-fashioned resort in the Adirondacks, at which he'd spent a week or two each summer since childhood. "Loons!" said the man. Though Bradley was hoping to be a writer, he didn't know what kind of birds loons were. The man described cabins at the edge of a lake. The dining room served three meals a day, he said, but the place wasn't fancy. "Nothing dressy," Bobbie had said.

With many miles still to drive on Route 28, Bradley and his mother turned off the Northway, which they had never seen before, at Warrensburg. Bobbie remembered long-ago trips on Route 9 to Lake George—the Burma Shave signs, the motor courts with their tiny separate houses. When Bradley was a baby, he and Bobbie—his father had already departed—were brought along on a vacation by Bobbie's sister Sylvia and her husband, Lou.

"Are you tired? Do you want to stop?" Bradley asked as they drove into Warrensburg. His mother sat trustingly beside him in her orange-pink turban, a color too harsh for her skin. He wanted to stop. As soon as he had a license, she was sure they could drive anywhere.

"I should take my pills," she said. He found a little lunch counter. They'd had lunch outside of Albany, but now they ordered pie and coffee. The waitress brought water. "In New York these days, you have to ask for water," Bobbie said.

Bradley hated watching her take the array of pills. She did it with abandon, like a starlet in a movie tossing down barbiturates after being left by her lover. Bobbie tipped her head back to gulp the water, but ate little of her lemon meringue pie.

They traveled west. They were going to a big lake, the site of the crime in the real story behind *An American Tragedy*. Bradley had read it at City College. He barely remembered it, yet it was still vivid for Bobbie, who said she'd read it in high school. "He rows her out onto the lake—" she said. "You know he's going to do it, but you're begging him, 'Don't!' "

After a while she slept, her lipsticked mouth open, her head tilted back. The turban was askew when Bradley glanced at her. When she awoke she resettled it, telling him, her voice a little groggy, "Want to hear something funny? When I first bought it and put it on, I thought, This isn't going to stay. Then I thought, I know what I need, a hat pin! Picture it, honey, picture it."

Bradley didn't want to picture it, but couldn't help it: as he steered around curves, his hands tight on the wheel, he imagined the fake pearl at one end, the sharp point at the other, not sliding harmlessly through tangled hair but straight into his mother's skull. "Horrible," he said. "Hush."

"Edwin didn't want to hear about it either." Edwin Friend was his mother's boyfriend. If they'd married, Bradley considered, would Edwin have been braver? He and Bobbie were the same age, but now he looked older than she did, old from fear, though he was well. Edwin drove Bobbie to doctors' appointments, waiting in his big car outside. "I don't like it when they call me Mr. Kaplowitz," he told Bradley. If his mother had become Bobbie Friend—such a lighthearted name—would she have gotten well, gotten her hair back: a tentative fuzz, then a soft crew cut, then thickening curls?

They reached the resort after five. When Bradley opened the car door, the air was pungent with the smell of the woods. His legs trembled as he walked to the office to check in, while Bobbie waited in the car. He put from his mind the knowledge that he'd have to drive as far again in only a week.

"The wood boy will come to your cabin every morning at six thirty," the woman in the office told him placidly.

"The what?" It sounded like an animal. Bradley looked past her as she sat in front of a window. The lake glittered in the late afternoon sun. He heard the whir of a motorboat, then saw it pulling a water-skier, who fell. The boat circled around for her.

"The wood boy. He's quiet." Water in the cabin, she said, was heated by the fireplace. The wood boy would start a fire each morning, so Bradley and his mother could take hot showers.

He got back into the car and described this arrangement to his mother, afraid she'd scold or grow petulant, feeling guilty for luring her here. The man in the bookstore hadn't mentioned the wood boy. But Bobbie laughed. "I wonder if the water really gets hot," she said. "Well, we can bathe in the lake." Bradley turned the key in the ignition one last time, and followed the instructions the woman had given him, driving slowly along a rutted road behind several widely separated log cabins, and at last parking the car. He turned off the engine and now let himself take in the silence, which was broken only by the light sound of the lake and the hum of the motorboat that pulled the water-skiers. He didn't bother with the suitcases, but helped his mother out, and they walked up some rough steps cut into the hill. His pants clung to his legs, but a breeze was already drying the sweat and making him cool.

The cabin had two bedrooms and a living room. In the bathroom, a tank for hot water felt cold to Bradley's touch. His mother hadn't followed him inside. She sank into an Adirondack chair on the porch, facing the lake. "Oh, honey, *look*," she called. He knew what she meant: it was what they had imagined: birch trees, evergreens, the lake, and dense woods beyond it. He was giddy with relief, carrying in their suitcases. Then he took her arm, and they walked on the lakeside path to dinner. That night they heard the reckless laughter of a loon.

Next day it rained. Sure enough, the wood boy was quiet, but Bradley awoke and listened. He waited in bed until he heard the boy leave, listening to the thump of logs being lowered to the floor and the sound of rain right above his head. Then he went into the living room, where a fire blazed from tinder.

After breakfast, Bobbie sat in her Adirondack chair on the porch, knitting a little sweater of fine yellow wool. One of Bradley's cousins was pregnant. Bradley sat in the other chair, looking at the gray lake and misty woods, digesting the unaccustomed breakfast—he'd had eggs and toast and potatoes. He was sleepy and bored, but content. It seemed that all he needed to do was keep Bobbie where she was, sitting back with her elbows close to her body, as the silvery blue knitting needles, with sixes on their bottoms, made their way, forward and back, through the looped and twisted yarn. She came to the end of a ball, which had slowly unraveled at her feet. She took another skein from her old pink quilted knitting bag, which Bradley had known most of his life. Now Bradley hitched his chair closer to his mother's so he could hold the skein on his outstretched wrists. As Bobbie wound her ball, Bradley tried to be even more helpful, tilting the skein this way and that by raising one arm slightly, then the other, his palms up. Without the yarn, he would have looked like someone *beseeching*. His mother's face looked young and enterprising as she worked, biting her lip slightly, concentrating. Finally the new ball—perfectly round, like something from a photograph on a calendar, including a kitten—was done.

"You're a good son," she said. "A better son than a mother."

"No," said Bradley. "A wonderful mother."

She was silent. With the ball in her lap, she tied its end to the short end of yarn coming off the yellow scrap that hung from the needles. Beginning to knit again, she said, "I'm sorry, honey."

"For what, what's wrong?" he said.

"Oh, nothing's wrong *here*, it's lovely," she said, as if he'd been the one who'd apologized. She glanced toward the lake, where mist rose in curls and streaks. "I mean—"

He knew now what she meant. "Hush," he said.

She was apologizing for what was going to happen. A good mother does not leave her son.

At lunch, Bradley ate onion soup for the first time. As he ate, he felt something alien in his mouth, and before he could decide not to, he'd swallowed it. It stuck, neither up nor down. Bobbie was talking about Edwin. "We could have married," she said. "We always *meant* to." Edwin had had a wife, a secret wife whom Bobbie somehow knew about. Then Edwin had divorced his wife. In the days when he'd claimed to be a bachelor, he said he couldn't marry because of his old, frail mother, and maybe that had been the truth all along, wife or no. His mother was still alive, managing alone in a smelly apartment in Red Hook, in her nineties. "But I'm not sorry!" Bobbie now said brightly.

Bradley didn't want to frighten her. He cleared his throat. Then, feeling self-conscious, he used his finger, but of course he couldn't reach whatever it was. At last he said, "I've got something caught in my throat," and his mother stiffened with alarm, her eyes wide open.

"I can talk, it's all right," Bradley said, but he couldn't endure the sensation, the sense of something caught. "Excuse me." He left the dining room. It was still raining lightly. Outside the building, he leaned over, panicky now, pressing his hands on his knees. He didn't care if he vomited, even if everyone in the dining room saw. He coughed and retched, but nothing came. Had the object moved? Was it blocking his windpipe? At last, as his eyes teared, he strained and brought up saliva, and something. He drew it out: a woody brown piece of the skin of an onion. His throat was swollen from his straining. He dropped the onion skin, wiped his eyes on his sleeve, and returned to the dining room. All the children in the room looked up as he entered. The waitress, a college girl, approached him. "Are you all right?"

"I'm fine," Bradley said. "I had a piece of onion skin lodged in my throat, but I coughed it up."

Outside, the rain seemed to be stopping, and blue areas appeared in the sky. Bradley gingerly ate a little more soup. "You're sure you're okay, honey?" Bobbie said.

"I'm sure."

While they ate dessert, the chef came out of the kitchen and walked over to their table. He was a skinny man in an apron and a chef's hat. "I just want to apologize," he said.

"Oh, it's nothing," Bradley said, wishing the incident would end.

"I saw the onion skin fall into the pot, but I just couldn't find it," he said. "I was afraid somebody would get it. Now, what were the odds it would be you?"

Puzzled, Bradley calculated the odds—one in about forty, except that not everyone had had soup. The chef's question seemed like one only Bradley could ask, but it pleased him.

Afterward, the weather cleared, but it was too cool to swim. Bradley had been adding logs to the fire all day, and for the first time since their arrival, the water tank was hot, so they both took showers. Then he proposed that they take out a canoe.

"I won't be much help," his mother said.

He had been to Boy Scout camp. "I think I can do it," he said.

The placid woman in the office was on the phone, so while he waited Bradley looked at a map of the lake that hung near her desk. Then she helped him carry a wooden canoe out of a shed and along the dock, dropping two life jackets into the bottom. No one was on the dock. The water-skiers, who had appeared as soon as the rain stopped, were gone. Bradley and the woman lowered the canoe into the water, while Bobbie stood by, her hand on the turban. There was a breeze. Then the woman held the rim of the canoe, kneeling on the dock in her blue jeans and leaning forward, while Bradley helped his mother into the bow, and settled himself in the stern with his paddle. The woman gave a brief underhand wave and turned back to the office.

Bradley remembered the stroke. Soon he found a rhythm, and in a short time he'd brought them a little distance from the dock, with the shore on his right. He struck out for deeper water, afraid of running aground.

As if continuing the conversation that had been interrupted at lunch, his mother said, "It's not always a bad thing, not to marry. At least I was married long enough to have you!"

"Yes," Bradley said to her back, not sure where this was going.

"Something I think about," she said. "You know, honey. The way you are. Now, I don't think there's anything wrong with it, you know. But not to marry, have children . . ."

"Yes," Bradley said, stroking hard. He steered past an inlet that looked narrow and shallow. The shore beyond it curved out, then in. He saw only a few houses in the dense evergreen woods.

"I think—if your father had stayed, if I'd been different, a different sort of mother. Maybe it wouldn't have happened."

Bradley was silent, considering what to say. He felt angry, and paddled hard but didn't speak until the feeling passed. "I can't imagine being different," he said then. "I was meant to be gay."

"Then it's all right?" she said, her back in a white sweater in front of him, her head looking ahead of her in its foolish turban.

"It's all right," he said.

They kept on, moving swiftly. Bobbie studied the lakeshore. "Maybe we'll see a deer coming to drink," she said. But a short time later she said, "Shall we go back, honey?"

He'd tired her. He turned the canoe. Now the shore was on his left. The resort was a long way off, past a peninsula he'd need to steer around. In front of him, his mother had folded her arms against the wind, which was now in their faces. It was hard to paddle, and he was tired. They'd gone too far.

"Are you cold?" he said.

"A little." He insisted on giving her his sweater, a woolen pullover. He took it off and held it out to her, but she wouldn't put it on over her white nylon cardigan. She took that off and handed it back to him. "Around your shoulders, at least. It will make a little difference." To please her, Bradley tied the white sleeves around his neck. The sweater did give him a little warmth. "Now, *you* wouldn't drown a girl in the lake," his mother said, and it took him a minute to remember *An American Tragedy*.

The lake looked entirely different from the other direction. Bradley remembered a brown boathouse, but he didn't see it. He came to the entrance to an inlet. Could the resort be *in* it? Had he come out into the wider lake, not realizing because the curve was gentle on that side? This inlet seemed too wide to be the one he'd bypassed, but he didn't enter it. Now and then they passed a dock, but never one that looked familiar. Children he'd seen swimming had disappeared. Bradley realized that he had no idea how their resort would look from the water. He couldn't remember how close to the shore the office was, whether the shed from which they'd taken the canoe would protrude from the trees. Maybe they'd already passed the resort. He paddled, rested, paddled. They made slow progress against the wind. Bradley looked at his mother, bulkier than she really was in the brown sweater, like a sturdier, more practical mother. She'd never wear brown. His throat was sore from the mishap at lunch. It felt as if he'd been crying, or as if he was getting a sore throat, the cozy kind that makes it permissible to shed responsibility and go to bed with tea and books. He'd liked that kind of illness as a child. Bobbie would bring him alphabet soup and chocolate pudding.

In his mind, Bradley again stood in the office, idly waiting for the woman who owned the resort to end her telephone call, staring at the map. Looking at the now cloudy lake, he struggled to form the map again in his mind, the kidney shape of the lake, with an extra lobe. He pictured the smudged black print, the lake's firm outline. The resort was marked with a star, closer to the western than the eastern end. It was on a wide, gently curved bay. Then came the inlet, then another bay, and then a peninsula.

"Someone will come along," his mother said, and he knew she knew they were lost.

"That's right," said Bradley, but he saw no boats. The tangled woods came down to the lake, and it seemed that nobody lived in them. Stroking and stroking, his tired hands gripping the paddle, his throat aching, Bradley brought his mother a little farther, then again a little farther, over the water.

A NOTE TO THE READER

This book's thirteen stories imitate in prose the thirteen stanzas of a double sestina, using repeated topics or tropes in something like the way a sestina—the poetic form described in the story "Brooklyn Sestina"—uses repeated words. In the changing order prescribed by the sestina pattern, each story includes a glass of water, a sharp point, a cord, a mouth, an exchange, and a map that may be wrong.

ACKNOWLEDGMENTS

I'd like to offer warm thanks to The Corporation of Yaddo and The MacDowell Colony, and to Paul Beckman, April Bernard, Susan Bingham, Kevin Callahan, Heather Gould, Donald Hall, Susan Holahan, Andrew Mattison, Ben Mattison, Edward Mattison, Jacob Mattison, Zoe Pagnamenta, Joyce Peseroff, Jennifer Pooley, Sandi Kahn Shelton, Emily Sklar, and my astonishing editor, Claire Wachtel.

My mother, Rose Eisenberg, told me an old story that became the basis for "I Am Not Your Mother." She believed unfailingly in my work, and read and reread it as long as her eyes and mind allowed. No daughter, no writer, could ask for more.